DEATH SHOOTS A BIRDIE

This Large Print Book carries the
Seal of Approval of N.A.V.H.

DEATH SHOOTS A BIRDIE

CHRISTINE GOFF

WHEELER PUBLISHING
An imprint of Thomson Gale, a part of The Thomson Corporation

THOMSON
—★—™
GALE

Detroit • New York • San Francisco • New Haven, Conn. • Waterville, Maine • London

THOMSON

GALE

LIBRARY OF CONGRESS CATALOGING-IN-PUBLICATION DATA

Goff, Christine.
  Death shoots a birdie / by Christine Goff.
    p. cm. — (Wheeler Publishing large print cozy mystery)
  "A Birdwatcher's Mystery"—T.p. verso.
  ISBN-13: 978-1-59722-561-8 (softcover : alk. paper)
  ISBN-10: 1-59722-561-4 (softcover : alk. paper)
    1. Bird watchers — Fiction. 2. Bird watching — Fiction. 3. Barrier islands
  — Georgia — Fiction. 4. Georgia — Fiction. 5. Large type books. I. Title.
  PS3607.O344D425 2007
  813'.6—dc22   2007014649

Published in 2007 by arrangement with The Berkley Publishing Group, a member of Penguin Group (USA) Inc.

Printed in the United States of America on permanent paper
10 9 8 7 6 5 4 3 2 1

To my dad, Harry McKinlay, who helped me explore the swamp.

ACKNOWLEDGMENTS

My deepest thanks to Lydia Thompson, artist and birder extraordinaire, who supplied me with insider information on the birds of Coastal Georgia; to the tour guides, who escorted my father and me through the swamp, for sharing their knowledge of the wildlife and legends of the Okefenokee; and to Suzanne Proulx for her friendship and expertise in all things writing.

Additional thanks to Gwen Shuster-Haynes, Margie Lawson, and the women of the "Think Tank" (Christine Jorgensen, Leslie O'Kane, Cheryl McGonigle, Kay Bergstrom, and Carol Caverly) for their unflagging help, support, and encouragement; and to Averill Craig for submitting the winning title for this novel.

And finally, I would like to thank my editor, Cindy Hwang, for her patience; Peter Rubie, my agent, for his unflagging confidence; and my family, my biggest cheerleaders, who continue to believe I can do anything — well, almost anything.

———

CHAPTER 1

Rachel Wilder studied Guy Saxby's photograph in the Hyde Island Birding and Nature Festival brochure, and compared it to the man standing near the bird feeders. He had the same square jaw, the same sharp eyes, and the same light hair, though he looked blond in the photograph and gray in the sunlight. She would swear it was him. Tamping down her excitement, she drew a deep breath of the humid Georgia air, and pushed back an errant curl.

"Rae, are you coming?"

"Lark!" Rachael called in a stage whisper, waving her hand in the universal signal for "Come here." "Come here!"

Her friend stood her ground. Anchored to the bottom step leading to the entrance of the Hyde Island Nature Center, Lark planted her hands on her hips. "What is it?"

Rachel gestured again, and Lark reluctantly stepped down. Rachel met her half-way.

"Isn't that Guy Saxby?"

"How should I know?" said Lark. "I've never met him."

"Lark, you have to have seen him at some point, or at least seen pictures of him." Guy Saxby was a big birder, huge, and so was Lark. Their paths must have crossed somewhere. "Look at his photograph."

Rachel shoved the brochure into Lark's hands. She looked down at the photo, then at the man nearby. "Now that's what I call a really old headshot."

"Granted. But is it him?"

Lark scrunched up her face and tipped her head sideways, her long blonde braid whipping side to side. "I think so."

"Yes." Rachel shot her arm into the air then dropped her elbow to her waist.

"He's the guy, isn't he? The one Kirk wants you to cozy up to?"

"In a manner of speaking."

Rachel had briefed her traveling companions on her assignment during the ride up from the airport. Lark Drummond, Cecilia Meyer, and Dorothy MacBean had flown in from Colorado to attend the Hyde Island Birding and Nature Festival. It had been two years since she'd seen them, and they

10

had been more interested in hearing about what she had been up to than what she had planned. They wanted to know how she liked living in New York. How well she liked her job. Was she in love with Kirk Udall?

To their credit, they had a vested interest. They were all there when she met him, during the investigation into his colleague's murder in Elk Park. A reporter for *Birds of a Feather* magazine had been murdered, and Rachel's aunt was implicated in the crime. Rachel had been staying with her. Together Rachel and Kirk, with the help of the Elk Park Ornithological Chapter, had cracked the case. She and Kirk had been dating ever since.

"He asked you to spy on the man," said Lark.

"Kirk didn't actually use the word *spy*."

But that was the gist. He had been all set to join them himself when the magazine decided to send him to Sri Lanka at the last minute. They wanted a piece on how bird populations weather natural disasters, which left *her* to ferret out Saxby's secret.

Kirk was doing an expose on Saxby, an icon in the birding world. As a young professor, he had written a book entitled *A Sacrifice of Buntings* about the plight of the painted bunting on the Eastern Seaboard

11

and his observations had proved prophetic. Now he was a world-renowned expert on endangered species, and set to unveil a new project. Something big. Something that would "rock the bird world." Kirk wanted the inside scoop.

"Now that we've identified the guy, no pun intended, can we go?" asked Lark. "Dorothy and Cecilia are already inside." Lark looked wilted in her jeans and flannel shirt, and Rachel felt a stab of sympathy. The others were dressed for Colorado weather. It was only late April, but the temperatures in Georgia were already into the eighties. At this point, all any of the Coloradoans cared about was air conditioning.

Rachel wasn't exactly dressed for bird-watching herself. She'd worn black silk crop pants and a tank top on the plane, but at least she was cool. "You go ahead. I'll follow you."

"Don't tell me. You're going to go and introduce yourself, aren't you?"

"In a manner of speaking."

Lark climbed the stairs while Rachel retrieved her binoculars from the car. Creeping up to stand beside Saxby without scaring the birds on the feeder, Rachel adjusted her binoculars.

A brightly painted bunting squatted at the base of the broken-down bird feeder, seemingly oblivious to the aesthetics of its surroundings. Georgia greenery touched the sky to the south and east. To the north and west were the parking lot and a Dumpster. Small and sparrow-sized, the bird kept a watchful eye as he ate, peering out from behind a scarlet eye ring and swiveling his blue-violet head side to side.

"Beautiful, isn't he?" asked Saxby.

Rachel kept her binoculars trained on the bird. "Gorgeous."

A light breeze molded the painted bunting's bright apple-green feathers flat to its back and ruffled its scarlet underparts as though underlining her statement. Behind him, two lime-green females twittered like schoolgirls enamored with a new beau.

Out of the corner of her eye, Rachel gave Saxby the once-over. Based on the gray that peppered his hair, he had to be in his mid-fifties, maybe twenty years older than she. Tanned and fit, he was of average height, average build. His shorts zippered at the knees, and he wore a state-of-the-art, long-sleeved, vented shirt straight out of the Big-Pockets catalog.

He seemed to sense her scrutiny, and returned it. "Are you from around here?"

13

he asked.

"No." She kept her answer short and simple. She figured it was obvious by the way she was dressed — no colorful T-shirt and shorts like the locals. "I'm from New York."

"City?"

The question sounded rhetorical, so she didn't answer.

"You're not down here for the festival, are you?"

Rachel lowered her binoculars. "Do you find that so hard to believe?"

"A pretty, young businesswoman . . ." He half-shrugged, then straightened and focused sharply on something beyond her. "Whoops! Here comes trouble."

He pointed, and Rachel glanced left. In a flash of rainbow colors, a second male painted bunting swooped into the trees, rousting the first male off the bottom of the feeder. Hopping up and along the pole, the feeder bird perched at the topmost point and belted out a song.

Saxby joined in with a husky baritone. "This land is my land. It's not your land."

Rachel grinned. He had scored a direct hit on the painted bunting psyche. It was one of the species Lark had said they would see on this trip, and Rachel had boned up on the bird. The males of the species were territorial, and had even been known to kill their competition in defense of their breeding ground. The females tended to choose the best provider, even if it meant sharing a mate. Obviously, the bird in control of the feeder had the edge.

The interloper dived out of the live oak, swooped past the Dumpster, and landed on the graveled driveway, cutting a swath past the wax myrtles. Pressing himself close to the ground, he shook out his wings.

"He's making a challenge!" Saxby raised his binoculars and twisted them into focus.

Rachel followed suit.

The painted bunting flitted across the Georgia dirt, and hopped a few inches closer. Defiantly, the feeder bird flaunted his scarlet rump and sang louder, his voice jerky and off-key. The females stopped eating and huddled closer together on the backside of the feeder.

In a riot of colors, the male birds flew. Rachel lost track of which bird was which as they fluttered their wings in each other's faces, grappling mid-air before tumbling to earth.

Rachel leapt forward. "We have to stop them before one of them ends up dead."

"What do you think you're doing?" yelled

Saxby. He grabbed her arm, but it was too late. The birds broke apart. One bird flew into the trees. The other hopped up on the feeder.

Saxby's body tensed. "Do you know how many people would kill for the chance you just had, to see two painted buntings in battle? Very few people ever have the opportunity to witness life in action like that."

Rachel felt her hackles go up. "One of them was sure to be hurt. It seemed only right to stop them."

Saxby looked disgusted. "Have you ever heard the saying 'survival of the fittest'? By interfering you've upset the ecological balance."

Rachel felt the heat rise to her cheeks. "I'm sorry. I just . . ."

Saxby's body language softened. "You're new to birding, aren't you?"

She nodded. She had started birding just three years ago, and only had the opportunity now and then. She'd been doing more serious birding with Kirk, but only for the past year.

"Well, what's done is done. I wouldn't worry about it if I were you." Saxby dangled his binoculars against his chest. "Besides, it looks like the older bird would have won."

Rachel frowned. "How can you be so sure?"

"Check out the face of the bird on the feeder. The incoming male was a young bird. The feeder bird bears a few scars. He's learned to defend himself in a turf war."

"By eliminating the competition?"

Saxby shrugged. "It works for him."

"That sounds a bit cavalier if death is the usual outcome."

"Not usual." He paused and studied her. "You disapprove. Is a fight to the death not romantic or idealistic enough for you? Sometimes life is like that."

Rachel wondered if Saxby's cynicism had to do with his age. Maybe it was time to change the subject. "You're Guy Saxby, aren't you?"

"In the flesh." He seemed pleased that she had recognized him.

"I'm Rachel Wilder."

"Rachel." He had just reached for her hand when a pretty brunette in a green Honda pulled up and tooted the horn. Squeezing Rachel's fingers, he nodded toward the vehicle. "My chariot awaits. Enjoy your stay on the island. Perhaps I'll see you at the festival."

Before Rachel could think of something clever to stop him, Saxby had walked away and climbed into the car.

The brunette gunned the engine and pulled away.

"Rae!"

Rachel turned and spotted Lark galloping back down the steps of the Hyde Island Nature Center.

The tall blonde lolled out her tongue, and fanned the collar of her flannel shirt. "Whew boy, it's hot. I'm ready to check into the hotel and change into my shorts."

Rachel nodded absently and watched the Honda speed away.

"Guy Saxby and friend?" asked Lark.

"Guy Saxby and driver." The girl was obviously too young to be his friend. Wasn't she?

"Did you learn anything?"

Rachel remembered his lecture and felt herself blush. "Nothing Kirk would be interested in."

"He didn't look anything like I'd expected," said Lark.

That struck Rachel as odd. "Why? What did you expect?"

"I don't know, someone more dashing. He has a reputation, you know. He *is* the Indiana Jones of the birding world."

Was she being facetious?

"Are you saying he doesn't look roguish

enough?"

"I just thought he'd be cuter, *younger,* that's all. More like . . ."

"Colin Farrell?" Rachel supplied.

"Right," said Lark, tugging at her long braid. "He's too Sean Connery-ish, minus the English accent and the sex appeal."

Lark sat down on a bench and Rachel sat down beside her. "What else do you know about him?"

"Not much."

"Come on, Lark. You have to know more than I do."

Kirk hadn't had much time to brief her. He'd given her Saxby's bio, and copies of two or three articles about the man. She knew he was a gifted writer and teacher, and that he'd once held the record for a "Big Year." The logic behind a competition to see the most North American birds in one year escaped Rachel, but Saxby's second book, *Chasing the Feather,* immortalized his adventure, detailing how he had stalked the birds and ended up besting James Vardaman's 1979 record of 699 species by one — a record that had stood until 1983.

"I know he travels a lot," offered Lark, tapping the heel of her boot against the iron leg of the bench. "He goes all over the place looking for birds. He's well known for his escapades, a few of which are captured on film."

"Like the Bouilia Incident?"

Lark nodded. "Except that time he didn't get the bird."

Rachel had read at least one account of that most recent adventure — a foray into the Western Australian outback in search of the elusive night parrot. The bird had been discovered in 1845 by a participant in Charles Stuart's central Australian expedition. By 1912, twenty-two specimens of the species were collected, after which the night parrot was never officially documented again. It was deemed a "lost species" until 1990, when participants of an Australian Museum–sponsored trip collected a night parrot carcass from the side of the road near Bouilia. The hunt was on.

Saxby flew down with a small contingent, but failed to document the species on film. He did, however, find another carcass in a low chinapod shrub, and succeeded in winning the Bouilia Desert Sands Camel Race. He even provided stunning images of himself crossing the finish line in first place — a small consolation to the University of Georgia for the thousands of dollars spent.

"There you two are," called Dorothy Mac-

Bean from the top of the stairs. "We've been looking all over for you."

Her sister, Cecilia, traipsed down the stairs behind her. "Are we ready to go?"

"More than," said Lark, flapping her flannel-clad arms against the muggy, Georgia heat. Her face shone a deep, cherry red, and Rachel experienced a pang of guilt for keeping her out in the heat.

Rachel pulled Lark to her feet and steered her toward the car. "We need to get you into some air conditioning. Plus I didn't tell you what we saw."

"What?" demanded Dorothy.

Cecilia fixated on the "we."

"You and who else?" she asked, looking at Lark.

"Rachel and Guy Saxby."

"*The* Guy Saxby?" blurted the sisters in unison.

Rachel stifled a laugh. She was reminded of *The Patty Duke Show* theme song — "They look alike, they walk alike, at times they even talk alike. You could lose your mind . . ." Except for the fact that Dorothy's favorite color was pink while Cecilia's was blue, they wore the same stylish clothes, had the same pale skin, the same gray-colored eyes, and the same ash-blonde perm, with a youthfulness that belied their sixty-plus years.

"You *are* aware that he is an eligible bachelor," said Cecilia, elbowing her sister.

"Don't even start." Dorothy held her fingers up in the sign of the cross.

"I have no idea what you're talking about," said Cecilia, feigning innocence. She had been trying to fix up her sister for years. Or, for that matter, anyone else who was single.

Rachel raised her own palms in surrender. "Don't look at me. I'm already taken."

"Count me out, too," said Lark. She was practically engaged to Eric Linenger.

"Well you girls might be spoken for, but I know one of us who's eligible." Cecilia eyeballed her sister.

In truth, thought Rachel, they were both single. Dorothy had never been married, and Cecilia had been widowed for nearly forty-five years.

As if reading her mind, Dorothy waggled two fingers in Cecilia's face.

"I was married."

Dorothy smirked at her sister. "And I've had lovers. It doesn't count."

Like a guppy out of water, Cecilia opened and shut her mouth several times until finally she blurted out, "Well, I've seen Saxby's picture, and I think he's cute. He would be perfect for you."

"Grow up, Cec."

"Don't tell me you don't agree, Dot. He's a real . . . what's that term you use, girls?" She looked to Rachel and Lark. "A real 'piece of eye candy.' "

"That would be my aunt Miriam's expression," said Rachel.

Cecilia shrugged, linking elbows with her sister. "Come on, admit it. Say you're interested."

Dorothy yanked her arm free. "He's too young for me. I probably have ten years on the man."

"Eight," said Cecilia.

"Besides, I've never even met him."

"We can remedy that." Cecilia beamed at Rachel. "She knows him."

Judging by Dorothy's expression, Rachel decided it was time for intervention. "Enough already, do you guys want to hear about what we saw or not?"

"We do," replied Dorothy and Lark in unison.

Rachel pointed to the birds on the feeder and recounted the challenge, the battle, and her blunder. When she was done, the four of them stood for a moment and admired the victor.

"Saxby was right," said Cecilia. "You

should never have intervened."

"It's okay, dear," said Dorothy. She tipped her head and smiled at the bird. "Do you know, the painted bunting's a life bird for me."

It was a life bird for Rachel, too, but with as many birds as Dorothy had seen, it was hard to believe this was the first painted bunting she had seen in her lifetime.

Cecilia whipped around, surprise etched in the wrinkles on her face. "It is not, Dot. We saw one on that trip we took to Florida when we were teenagers."

"No, it doesn't count. This is the first one I've seen since I started counting."

"What's wrong with counting the first one you saw?" asked Cecilia. "I did."

"Then you're cheating."

"By whose rules?"

"By the rules of the American Birding Association," said Dorothy, "which clearly state that the recorder must be able to identify by distinguishing characteristics either visually or audibly the bird they are listing. That means, you can't take someone else's word for it. By my recollection, neither one of us had any idea what birds we were looking at back then. We were taking Mother's word for it."

"Except we both know now that *is* what

we were looking at back then. There isn't another bird anywhere in the world like the painted bunting."

"It's still against the rules," said Dorothy, "and I'm not counting it. Until now, that is."

Rachel glanced at Lark. Why were the sisters bickering like this? They liked to rib each other, but never to this extent.

As if reading her mind, Lark shrugged and tipped her head toward the car.

"Oh, my," said Cecilia, "You certainly are a stub—"

"So now you've both seen one," said Rachel, picking up on Lark's lead and curious about how many birds Dorothy had seen in her lifetime. "How many does that make on your life list, Dorothy?"

"Six hundred."

"That's a significant number of birds," said Rachel. The American Birding Association North American checklist only listed 921 species, which meant Dorothy had seen nearly two-thirds of all the bird types documented in the continental United States.

"I have six hundred and two," said Cecilia.

"Using questionable listing practices." Dorothy sniffed. "It only affords me better opportunities than you for new birds on this trip."

"A two-bird difference," said Lark, waggling a peace sign in Dorothy's face. "That's the sum net difference between your counts. What's up with you? You two are acting like three-year-olds, or worse, like two Phoebe Snetsingers about to duke it out in the parking lot."

Cecilia pulled up, and fluffed her short, curly hair. "Maybe Dorothy is, but I'm not that old."

Rachel had read about Phoebe Snetsinger. Introduced to birding in her thirties, she had been diagnosed with terminal cancer at age fifty and been given one year to live. Instead of therapy, she had started birding with a passion, defying her prognosis and dying at the age of sixty-eight in a car accident in Madagascar shortly after viewing an extremely rare helmet vanga. As far as Rachel knew, she still held the world record for listing the most birds.

"We're both sixty-something," said Dorothy.

"You're older."

"You're fatter."

Cecilia tugged at the hem of her blue shirt. "We wear the same size."

"But I'm taller."

26

Lark opened the front passenger's seat door. "Can we just go?"

"Wait," said Cecilia. "The bunting is singing again."

The four of them snatched up their binoculars and moved back toward the feeder. The interloper was sitting on a branch in the trees. The feeder bird was flaunting his scarlet rump.

The interloper swooped to the ground and shook out his wings.

The birds flew, and this time Rachel did nothing but watch, her grip tight on the binoculars.

Talons scrabbled. Beaks jabbed.

A jab to the throat drew blood.

Another jab left the young male down.

Rachel trained her binoculars on the bird. It took a last ragged breath as its life blood seeped into the ground.

CHAPTER 2

The bird's death put a damper on things.

Piling into the car, Rachel blasted the air conditioning. The cool air worked like a salve. She felt the tension ease out of her body, and once again enjoyed the view.

The road to their hotel wound past the south beaches, a small shopping center, the tennis courts, and a stretch of golf course. On their left, small beach houses nestled in suburban grids under a pine canopy. To the right, mansions sprawled on expansive lawns, shaded by giant oak, pine, and magnolia trees.

According to Rachel's guide book, the grand houses were remnants of a majestic era. In the 1880s, a man named Harry McKinlay, the descendant of a wealthy Hyde Island plantation owner, dreamed of creating a winter retreat for wealthy northerners. Peddling images of a Southern island paradise, he developed interest from members of New York's elite society while buying up the remaining parcels of island land. Then in 1886, he sold the island to a corporation of the world's wealthiest millionaires. And so the Hyde Island Club was born.

For sixty years, millionaires flocked to the island, interested in finding a spot for rest, relaxation, and privacy. Combining one-sixth of the world's wealth, there was no limit to the extravagance or exclusivity of the club. The island, being accessible only by yacht, became a place where secret meetings were held and history was made.

For McKinlay, maintaining the island's natural beauty and preserving its wild areas for hunting and fishing became a priority. For more than sixty years, Hyde Island was spared from the rapid land-altering activities taking place on other coastal islands. The "cottages," social halls, stables, service buildings, and nine-hole golf course took up less than 10 percent of the island's upland acreage. They inhabited the river side so the dwellings created little need for beach development contributing greatly to the island's preservation.

"Check it out," said Lark.

Ahead of them, the clubhouse loomed. Designed in American Queen Anne style, a large turret dominated the roof line. Extensive verandas, bay windows, and extended chimneys added to the overall asymmetrical design. Yellow-painted brick, black tile shingles, and white trim cast a decidedly Victorian air.

"You're sure this is the right place?" asked Dorothy.

"It's a fair trade," said Lark. "I met the proprietors through the Association of Historic Hotel Owners. They are planning on visiting Elk Park this summer with their family."

A few years ago, Lark had traded her trust fund for a Victorian hotel near Rocky Mountain National Park named The Drummond. Originally owned by her grandfather, the hotel had 130 guest rooms and came with a thirty-two-room "Winter Hotel," a carriage house, a concert hall, an eighteen-hole golf course, and a ghost. With the stroke of a pen, Lark had gone from privileged socialite to working stiff.

Now she'd finagled them a heck of a deal for a couple of rooms.

"Whoa, what's going on up here?" asked Lark.

At the turn in to the club, people lined the road on all sides. Mostly locals, Rachel figured, by the looks of them. The majority

30

were dressed in T-shirts, shorts, and tennis shoes or flip-flops. One or two wore more expensive birder clothing. A tall man with long, dark hair and a tie-dyed T-shirt appeared to be their leader.

Rachel slowed the car and put on her blinker.

The protest leader signaled his troops like a choir master, and they chanted in chorus, "No land swap. No land swap." Their signs read things like: BOYCOTT THE HYDE ISLAND CLUB!, NO LAND SWAP!, and SAVE THE PAINTED BUNTINGS!

"Oh my, they seem unhappy about something."

Rachel drove slowly through the crush of protestors and pulled up in front of the hotel. Tossing the keys to the valet, she pointed and asked, "What's all that about?"

He handed her a claim check for the car. "Nothing to worry about, ma'am."

Ma'am? Since when had she become a ma'am?

"I'll bring your luggage inside."

Rachel followed the others up the steps, casting a last glance at the crowd at the end of the drive swarming a light blue Lexus. Inside, a tall, stunning woman with a short dark bob greeted them in the foyer. Her brown-and-white polka-dotted sundress brushed against her tan calves, and her matching brown stilettos clicked on the polished wood floor. It was like a scene out of *Pretty Woman.*

"Lark, darling," said the woman, extending her hand. "You made it. How was your trip?" She leaned forward and pecked the air near Lark's ear.

"Patricia," said Lark, introducing the rest of them. "Patricia and her husband, Nevin Anderson, own the hotel."

Patricia beamed. "We are so glad you're here."

"What was that crowd at the entrance to the club all about, Pat?"

"Patricia. And that is nothing to worry about." Patricia's voice carried a hard edge, though her lips continued to be set in a smile.

Obviously the party line, thought Rachel.

Retrieving two sets of keys off the reservation counter, Patricia waved them toward the stairs. "Come, come, you must be ready to freshen up. We've put you in two adjoining club suites. That way you'll each have your own bed, and a little more room."

She led them up the stairs — a winding, carved affair, with plush wool carpet padding the steps. The walls were painted a pale yellow, and dark-framed portraits of the original owners hung on the wall.

"Your rooms are here, in the west wing."

Lark and Rachel took the first suite — a beautifully appointed room with café au lait–colored walls, floral bedspreads, two antique four-poster beds, and a sitting area complete with a loveseat, TV, a small Queen Anne's table, and two chairs. Two doors opened off the sitting area — one into the bathroom, the other into Dorothy and Cecilia's room, a mirror image of the one occupied by Rachel and Lark.

"I hope this will be adequate," gushed Patricia, crossing to the bay window and throwing open the shutters. Outside the front lawn rolled toward the yacht basin. The view was spectacular, marred only by the line of protestors in the distance.

"It's fabulous," said Lark.

Patricia's dark, wide-set eyes eased over Lark's flannel shirt, her jeans, and her boots. "Well, I'm sure the Drummond has its own . . . rustic charm."

That sounded like a put-down. Rachel shot Lark a glance.

Lark's expression darkened.

Patricia smiled.

Nothing like starting off on the wrong foot.

Rachel washed away the travel dust while

the rest of them unpacked and changed. Slipping into her T-shirt and shorts, she shed the trappings of the city and stepped into vacation mode — a mode it sometimes took days to acclimate to. Lip gloss in place of lipstick, bug lotion in place of perfume, and red hair swooped up in a messy ponytail versus a more professional coif. It was a start. Now she just had to work on her attitude.

An hour later, they were back in the car headed for the Hyde Island Convention Center. As she drove, Rachel soaked in the island's opulence. Mansions posing as summer cottages gave way to small neighborhoods of year-round homes. The lush grass and foliage of the housing development morphed into the greens of the golf course, and then she could see the dunes. White hedgerows sprigged with grasses and littered in driftwood gave way to a wide swath of beach. Sunshine shimmered on the water, and the smell of salt and magnolias tinged the air.

The convention center was perched on the edge of the dunes. Situated on the south side of the island, the back deck of the two-story, ranch-style building commanded a spectacular view of the Atlantic Ocean, making the center a choice location for most major island events. Proms, conferences, weddings, even funerals, were commonplace. This week, the building was divided in half: One wing welcomed the Hyde Island Birding and Nature Festival; the other, the Lucy Bell Cosmetic Convention.

Rachel turned into the driveway, braked the rental car, and coasted through the parking lot. Lucy Bell Cosmetic banners hung on both sides of the main entrance, and a gaggle of well-heeled women in stockings and suits clustered in front of the two sets of large double doors.

"Are you sure we're in the right place?" Rachel asked, tugging at the hem of her T-shirt. "If so, I'd say we're a tad underdressed."

"This is right," Lark insisted. "Our entrance is over there." She pointed toward the east side of the building and a smaller set of doors covered with a green awning. Near the curb stood a large clapboard sign mounted with the official Hyde Island Birding and Nature Festival poster.

"We're early," said Dorothy. "That's why there aren't more birders around."

Rachel checked her watch. Four o'clock. Registration didn't open until five.

"We could take a walk on the beach," she suggested.

"Or maybe they'll let us register early," said Cecilia. "That would save us from having to stand in line."

Lark nodded. "It's worth a try. The last I heard, twelve hundred people had preregistered for the festival, and they're expecting another thousand to walk through the doors."

This was Rachel's first birding extravaganza, but she found those numbers hard to believe. "Twenty-two hundred attendees? That's a heck of a lot of birdwatchers."

"Give it a few years," said Lark.

"I was being facetious."

"Park there," said Cecilia and Dorothy.

At the others' urging, Rachel squeezed the car between two pale blue Cadillac convertibles and the four of them piled out. They made it less than ten yards across the parking lot before being engulfed by a wave of Lucy Bell Cosmetic conventioneers.

"Hello," chirped a perky brunette in a pink suit. In spite of the heat waves rising up from the pavement, she looked cool and fresh.

"How are you ladies doing today?" asked a blonde with artfully applied makeup and a Doris Day haircut, who circled in behind.

"Fine," answered Rachel, patting the neckline of her cotton T-shirt and straightening the hems of her shorts. It was amazing how a well-dressed woman could make another woman self-conscious. *Avoid eye contact,* she thought, hoping the others picked up her ESP.

The brunette stepped into her path. "Are you all part of the birding thing?"

"Oh, my," said Cecilia, fingering her hair. "Could you tell?"

The brunette and Rachel exchanged glances.

"We were just over there," said the brunette. "And we were thinking that after a day out in the field you all could probably use a facial or a good foot massage."

"Lucy Bell has a special cinnamon foot cream," piped up the blonde. "It's delicious."

"It's edible?" asked Rachel. She glanced at Lark. *Tell me this isn't real.*

"In fact," the blonde chirped, "we've arranged it with the conference coordinator to let us set up a chair in the vending area starting tomorrow. Isn't that sweet?"

The brunette shoved a piece of paper into Rachel's hand. "Here's a discount coupon." She passed some out to the others, then looked them all up and down. "We also do total makeovers."

"Thanks." Rachel pushed past her, feeling

slightly offended. Lark and Dorothy followed her, but Cecilia lagged behind.

"Come on," ordered Dorothy.

"A foot massage sounds nice."

Not when the foot cream costs ten dollars an ounce.

Rachel dropped back, smiled at the Lucy Bell girls, and propelled Cecilia onto the curb. Once they were out of earshot, she whispered, "Take it from a New Yorker: Never stop and chat with anyone handing out flyers."

For all its outside glamour, the registration area inside the convention hall looked like any other. Gray industrial carpeting blanketed the floor, and white walls climbed to a high ceiling. Toward the back wall, two men were setting up folding chairs and draping long tables in burgundy and white. Near the front of the foyer, three people busied themselves stuffing canvas bags with magazines, literature, and birding tchotchkes.

Rachel dropped her Lucy Bell flyer in the nearest trash receptacle and stepped up to the table with Lark. The man closest to them glanced up.

"We're not open yet," he said. "We don't open 'til five."

He sounded like Dorothy, thought Rachel. Strident. "We know we're early, but —"

Lark elbowed her in the ribs. "Any chance you could make an exception for us?"

The man looked from one to the other. "If we did that, we'd have to make an exception for everybody."

"Oh for heaven's sake, Harold, help the girls," said one of the women, a dark-haired matronly type with an ample bosom. She pushed him toward several open boxes of envelopes. "What are your last names?"

Grudgingly, he pulled their registration envelopes, while the woman handed each of them a badge holder and a canvas bag. "Your tickets and name tags are inside the envelope," she explained. "Check and make sure that you have tickets for every field trip, workshop, and banquet you signed up for. You may have gotten your second choice. We had so many registrations a few of the field trips filled up fast."

They thanked her, and checked their tickets. The four of them had lucked out. They each had been assigned their number-one field trip choices — Sapelo Island on Monday, Little St. Simons on Wednesday, and the Okefenokee Wildlife Refuge canoe trip on Friday. Their workshop schedules varied. Rachel had signed up for the all-day

"Digiscoping Workshop" on Thursday while Dorothy, Cecilia, and Lark had chosen more esoteric classes such as "Identifying Georgia's Shorebirds" and "Listing for the Advanced Birder." All of them had banquet tickets for Thursday, Friday, and Saturday nights.

"It looks like everything's here," said Rachel, stuffing the envelope into her bag. "Thanks again." She had started toward the entrance, when a tall man banged through the double doors.

"Where the hell is Evan?" he demanded, jostling her aside. When he slammed his fist on the table, Rachel jumped.

The man brandished a program at the volunteers. "*This* is bullshit. I want to talk to Evan, *now!*"

"Calm down, Dr. Becker," said Harold, pulling his skinny frame to its full height. "Trudy's going to get him," he said, gesturing for the woman who'd intervened on their behalf to go find Evan.

Rachel decided that, judging by the reaction of the registration staff, Becker was important. He didn't look familiar to her. Like Saxby, he was decked out in the latest birding fashion — vented shirt, pants, and a khaki vest covered with pockets. Tall, with brown hair and smallish brown eyes, he

40

paced the length of the registration table, tugging at the corners of a thin, brown moustache.

Rachel looked at the others. Dorothy and Cecilia stood with their mouths slightly agape, swiveling their heads as he paced back and forth, like Taco Bell Chihuahuas at a tennis match. Lark returned Rachel's gaze and shrugged.

Finally Trudy returned with a wiry, gray-haired man.

"What's the problem, Paul?"

Becker jabbed the cover of the program with his finger. "We had a deal. I was supposed to have the Saturday keynote slot, and then I open up this to discover you've listed me on Friday and given my slot to Saxby."

The man named Evan paled. "Look, Paul, the committee felt —"

"Don't give me that crap," said Becker. "You're the conference coordinator. It's your decision."

"Unfortunately, the committee —"

Becker threw down the booklet. "I'm the headliner this year. I'm the draw. Either I speak on Saturday night or you can take me off the program."

"You don't mean that."

"By God, I do."

A small group of volunteers had gathered, including Saxby, who must have been in the back.

"What's going on here?" he asked Rachel.

"You know damn well what's going on," Becker responded, spinning around to face him. "For some unfathomable reason, you've been given my keynote slot."

Saxby looked at Evan.

The man raised up his bony arms. "The commit—"

"Screw the committee," hollered Becker. "You promised me Saturday night when you brought me on board. Do you intend to honor the agreement or not?"

Evan tented his fingers and pressed them against his lips. After what seemed an interminable time he lowered them to a prayer position. "You're right, Paul. I did promise you the slot. But —" He raised his hand to silence Becker. "That was before we brought Guy on board. Once he had agreed to attend, the *committee*" — he stressed the word — "felt that Saturday night should be his. I'm sorry, but it's out of my hands."

"Then I'm gone."

"Hold on a minute," said Saxby, stopping Becker midway to the door. Reaching out, he laid a hand on Becker's arm. Becker sloughed it off.

"Paul, listen to me," said Saxby. "There are a lot of people looking forward to hearing you speak. You can't just leave. What does it matter if you speak Friday or Saturday? The turnout is always the same."

"Then you take Friday."

There was a collective gasp, and the entire room full of people seemed to suck in their breath.

The silence stretched.

Saxby's eyes narrowed, and he worked his jaw.

Becker waited, a smile twitching at the corners of his mouth. "Well?"

"Why not?" said Saxby. "Like I said, Friday or Saturday, what does it matter?"

"It matters to me," replied Becker.

Based on Saxby's expression, Rachel figured it mattered to him, too. But what could he do after making a statement saying the night didn't matter?

"What do you say, Evan?" asked Saxby. "The programs and brochures are already printed. I'm afraid it might upset the commit—"

"Ah, to hell with the committee," said Evan. "I'll just announce the change, and we can slip something into the packets." Evan clapped him on the shoulder. "This is extremely generous of you, Guy."

"Yes," said Becker. *"Generous."*

His sarcasm didn't escape any of them, and Dorothy was still fuming a few minutes later when they were back at the car.

"What a horrible man!"

"Now, Dot," scolded Cecilia. "You don't know why he wanted the Saturday-night slot. For all you know, he may have a very good reason."

"Such as wanting the limelight?"

Now who was being sarcastic. Rachel bit down on her lip.

"I know bad behavior when I see it," continued Dorothy. "Someone needs to teach that young man some manners."

"Who was he, anyway?" asked Lark, flipping backward through the pages of her program. "He must have a bio in here somewhere."

"If he's a keynote speaker it should be near the front," said Rachel starting the car, and backing out of the parking slot.

Lark stopped flipping.

"It says here that 'Paul Becker is a wildlife research biologist for the University of Georgia,' " she read. " 'A graduate of the university, he worked with the U.S. Fish and Wildlife Service for twelve years, before returning to UGA to head up a specialized ten-year research study on painted buntings.' " Lark looked up. "That means he works in Saxby's department at the university."

"Which explains the animosity," said Rachel, turning the car onto the main road.

"How so?" asked Cecilia.

"Because Saxby's the department head," answered Dorothy.

"Right," said Rachel. "And I'm willing to bet he's tenured. Becker wouldn't be if his bio is correct. He worked for the government for twelve years, and he's got to be ten years younger than Saxby."

"At least," said the others.

"Professional jealousy," murmured Cecilia.

"Or any number of things." Rachel flipped the turn signal, and turned left onto Hyde Island Club Road. "Project funding, personalities, office space —"

"Notoriety," added Dorothy.

"That, too," said Rachel. "What else does it say about him?"

Lark bent over the program. " 'Becker has received numerous awards for his efforts on behalf of Georgia's endangered species. An avid birder with an emphasis on North American species, his life list totals 825.' "

"Oh my!" blurted Cecilia. "He certainly

has my record beat."

"*Our* records," corrected Dorothy.

Lark stuck the program between the center console and the seat. "Everyone's records. That number puts him within reach of the top ten listers in America."

Dorothy sniffed. "Do we care?"

Rachel thought back to her conversation with Saxby about the painted buntings. "I wonder how many birds Saxby has listed. He seems like the type of guy who likes to win."

Rachel took a roundabout way back to the hotel, circling the island to get the lay of the land. White-sand beaches to the south gave way to driftwood to the north, then salt marshes. Gulls, wood storks, cattle egrets, and pelicans gave way to great blue herons and greater yellowlegs.

When they arrived back at the hotel, Saxby stood at the front desk talking to the clerk.

"But the Becker reservation is a couple," the clerk was saying.

"I don't care," Saxby replied. "I want a room at least as good as the one he has, or better."

"We're booked solid, sir. I assure you, I don't have any available rooms, and it's not in my power to move any of our guests. I apologize if your present accommodations are unsatisfactory —"

"Exactly," Saxby said. "My present accommodations are unsatisfactory. I don't intend to accept second best here."

The desk clerk frowned. "One moment, sir."

The desk clerk picked up the phone, held a quiet conversation, and a minute later handed Saxby a new key. "This room is in the west wing."

Our wing, thought Rachel.

"It's the first suite to the left on the third floor. Our best," said the clerk. "I'll send up a porter to move your things."

"Thank you." Saxby's response was polite, if equally stiff. He half turned, spotted the women, and smiled, nodding recognition to Rachel as they passed.

"They're both jerks," said Rachel.

"Who, the clerk?" asked Dorothy.

"No. Becker and Saxby."

"Becker, yes," agreed Dorothy as they ascended the stairs. "But Saxby just got rooked out of the Saturday keynote. Maybe Evan told him to ask for an upgrade for his magnanimous gesture."

Rachel looked askance. "Then why didn't he just say so?"

CHAPTER 3

The rest of the evening went smoother. Dinner was a quiet affair, and they all steered clear of talking about the scene at the registration desk. Instead, conversation swirled around common friends, Elk Park, and the excitement each felt about the next day's trip to Sapelo Island.

Retiring early, Rachel showered, donned her pajamas, and propped herself up in bed with the program and her guidebook while Lark brushed out her hair.

"This reminds me of when we were kids having sleepovers at the Drummond," said Rachel.

They had been friends growing up, spending their summers together in Elk Park, playing in the meadow between Bird Haven and the Drummond Hotel. After Lark's grandfather died, she had stopped coming, but years later they had reconnected. The same summer Rachel had met Kirk Udall.

"Do you have any secrets to share?" asked Rachel.

Lark blushed.

"Dish," demanded Rachel, scooting toward the edge of the bed.

"Eric and I are talking about getting married."

"Really?" Rachel clapped her hands in excitement, and Lark brought her finger to her lips.

"Shhhhh." She gestured toward the adjoining door. "We haven't told anyone yet."

"You will call me as soon as it happens?"

"Of course," said Lark, "when, *if,* we make plans. Right now, we're just exploring the idea." She went back to brushing her hair. "What about you and Kirk?"

Rachel settled back against the headboard. *What about me and Kirk?* "We're friends, that's all."

Friends who sleep together on occasion, and who spend a lot of time together. But after her disastrous first marriage, Rachel wasn't sure she ever wanted to hear someone utter the *M* word again. Not in relation to her.

"Remember who you're talking to, Rae."

"What's that old saying, 'once burned, twice shy'?"

"Don't let your experience with Roger get

in the way of your happiness. You'd only be letting him win that way."

It was hard to argue with logic. Still, Lark didn't know how awful it was to go through a divorce. It had taken her a year to settle things with Roger, and that had tainted her "friendship" with Kirk.

The silence stretched.

Finally Lark changed the subject. "What does the program say about Sapelo Island?"

Rachel felt a surge of relief that the conversation had moved on, and she picked up the booklet. "Do you want me to read from the top?"

Lark nodded.

" 'State-owned and largely undeveloped, Sapelo Island is considered the midpoint of Georgia's barrier islands, the location of the oldest remnant of Indian activity, and the probable site of the first European settlement in Georgia.' " Rachel glanced up from the program. "We have history."

"Keep going."

" 'The majority of land was privately owned until the establishment of the University of Georgia's Marine Institute in 1953, followed by the R. J. Reynolds Wildlife Management Area in 1969 and the Sapelo Island National Estuarine Research Reserve in 1973.' " Rachel looked up again. "We have more history."

This time Lark made a twirling motion with her finger.

" 'Descendants of the Geechee culture still inhabit the island community of Hog Hammock. . . .' "

"What's the Geechee culture?" asked Lark.

Rachel lowered the program. "I read about them in my guidebook, *Denton's Guide to Coastal Georgia*. They're the descendants of freed slaves who used to work the coastal island plantations of South Carolina and Georgia. They're called Gullah in South Carolina."

Lark set down her brush and began plaiting her hair. "What does it say about birds?"

Rachel skimmed through the write-up. "It talks about the land, then . . . oh, here. 'A mix of woodland, grassland, marsh, shore and seabirds can be seen here year-round.' Then we're into 'Recommended Needs.' " Rachel set aside the program, and scooted down in the bed.

"Okay, so we should see some terns, some buntings, and hopefully some eastern warblers tomorrow," said Lark, her voice tinged with excitement. "Does the program say who the trip leaders are?"

Rachel reached for the program, and rescanned the page. " 'Recommended Needs,' 'Trip Rigor,' 'Leaders!' Evan Kearns and —"

"Who?"

Rachel handed Lark the program. "Guy Saxby."

Five a.m. came early the next morning. Rachel sat on the edge of the bed, rubbing her eyes, and watched Lark bustle around the hotel room.

"You are a definite morning person," Rachel said. This was her time zone and she was dragging, while Lark virtually bubbled with energy.

"I'm serious, Rae. Birding buses don't wait for anyone, not even trip leaders. They'll leave without us. Do you have all your stuff?"

Rachel pulled her fingers through her hair and thought about it. She was wearing a long-sleeved shirt over her tank top, *check,* long pants, *check,* socks and tennis shoes, *check, check.* Her binoculars were inside her backpack along with a field guide, a Georgia checklist, insect repellent, sunscreen, water, snacks, and some money for the ferry and lunch. As an afterthought, she added her travel guide and the program with the field trip description.

"How about your name badge and your trip ticket?" asked Lark.

Those were items Rachel had forgotten.

Snatching her badge holder off the bedside table, she slipped it around her neck and stuffed the ticket in behind the name tag. *Check, check.*

She caught a glimpse of herself in the mirror, stopped, and scooped her auburn curls into a ponytail, feeding it through the hole in the back of her cap and forcing upon it some semblance of control. Swiping a final layer of sunscreen across her nose, she said, "Okay, I'm ready."

"Then let's go."

The hallway was empty, which meant either everyone else was sleeping or the two of them were running quite late. Based on Dorothy's pacing of the foyer, Rachel guessed the latter.

"There you two are," said Cecilia, shoving a cup of coffee into Rachel's hands. "We need to hurry."

Lark drove. Rachel waved at the one or two protestors standing at the end of the drive, coffee in hand. Five minutes later they pulled into the parking lot at the convention center.

"That's the bus. You had better step lively." A volunteer, wearing a beige sweat-shirt embellished with the conference logo, pointed them toward the bus — a retired Greyhound, painted green, with OKEFENO-KEE SWAMP TOURS stenciled on the side in hot turquoise.

Rachel climbed the steps and found herself standing in an aisle between two rows of worn, cloth-covered seats. Birders packed the inside. Birding scopes, backpacks, and jackets were jumbled into the overhead storage, and Guy Saxby sat front and center, holding out a hand for their tickets.

"Glad you could join us, ladies."

Rachel worked to extricate her ticket from behind her name badge with one hand. Giving up, she tried handing her coffee cup to Dorothy, who kept staring at Saxby and wouldn't respond. She must not have read her program book. "Dorothy!"

The woman startled, a pinkish stain flooding her face. "Sorry," she mumbled, taking the cup.

Rachel suppressed a smile.

Dorothy continued to preen while Rachel fished out her ticket. The older woman shifted her weight from side to side, fluffed her hair with her free hand, and chattered nonstop to Cecilia about how excited she was to go on this particular field trip.

"Here you are," said Rachel, handing

Saxby her ticket. She waited for Dorothy to notice she was ready to take back her cup.

"Thank you," replied Saxby, gesturing for her to pass.

"You're welcome." She signaled Dorothy to give back her cup. Dorothy just kept up the patter.

"I can take that back now," said Rachel.

Dorothy's face grew redder.

By the time Rachel had recaptured her coffee, Lark had moved to the back of the bus. Rachel followed, winding her way through the elbows that jutted out into the aisle. Behind her, Dorothy pulled Cecilia into the empty front seat reserved for the second trip leader.

"Check it out," said Rachel, slipping past Lark to sit next to the window. "Dorothy has a crush on Saxby."

"Dorothy and half the women on the bus."

There was truth in that statement. A lot of the female birders had crammed themselves into the front seats, where they twittered like a sacrifice of female buntings lusting after the feeder bird. In the back around Lark and Rachel sat mostly couples and a few stray men.

Rachel watched Dorothy laugh at something Saxby was saying, and then watched Saxby smile. It seemed like he was going to let them stay in the reserved spots. Settling back against her seat, Rachel closed her eyes and listened to the snatches of conversation floating around her. From what she could tell, the birders comprised an eclectic bunch — young and old, rich and poor, experienced and relative beginners. Based on some of the terms being bantered about, several were clearly professionals — people who either specialized in bird-related areas or had made birding their postretirement profession. Across the aisle were a housewife and her daughter, a student from the University of Georgia. A doctor, a dentist, and a lawyer rounded out the seating, with at least one pseudo–auto mechanic giving someone directions on changing the oil in a BMW. This was a bus full of people, Rachel decided, who came from all over, united by only one thing — a desire to see birds.

A burst of static caused Rachel to open her eyes. The passengers quieted, and Saxby rekeyed the mike. "Hello."

"Hello," parroted the groupies in the front.

"Are we ready to go birding?"

"Yes," replied the groupies.

"I can't hear you in the back. Can you all hear me?"

Heads bobbed.

"I asked, are we ready to go birding?" Saxby raised his voice, and held out the microphone.

"Yes," responded the busload.

Rachel sipped her coffee.

As if on command, the old Greyhound sputtered to life. A white mist spewed from the vents, and a murmur rippled through the bus. Saxby leaned toward the driver — a tall, well-built man with a short brush haircut. He grinned into the rearview mirror.

"It's okay, folks," he said, in a deep Southern twang. "It's just the swamp cooler kicking in."

The ladies in the front giggled.

Saxby smiled. "This is Dwayne," he explained, gesturing toward the driver. "One announcement, Evan Kearns can't be with us today. He was scheduled to be my coleader, but some changes have occurred in the weekly program, and he needed to stay behind and orchestrate things."

Rachel and Lark exchanged glances.

"We've been more than compensated for his loss, however. We have several people taking this trip who are more than qualified to take his place." Saxby pointed out two men seated in front of Lark and Rachel. "Would you two mind raising your hands, gentlemen? Folks, if you have any questions about what you're seeing and you can't find me, these are the guys to ask."

The bus lurched forward, and Saxby grabbed for a handrail. Rachel instinctively checked her watch. *A definite on-time departure!*

"Now, we have a half-hour's drive to the ferry," said Saxby, "so sit back, relax, and let me tell you a little bit about Sapelo Island."

His voice droned on with information straight out of the program book, and Rachel leaned over to Lark, keeping her voice low so no one could hear her. "He's really more Sean Connery-ish than you think."

"Oh, please."

Rachel put her finger to her lips. "Seriously, he's got the nicely trimmed moustache, the beard, and his eyes are to die for."

Lark wrinkled her nose. "Right, if you're Dorothy's age."

"Is that what bugs you, his age?"

Lark checked to see if anyone was listening, and then leaned closer to Rachel. "Remember how I said he had a reputation?"

"The Indiana Jones of birding."

"Right, well the same goes with the ladies, and rumor has it he likes them young."

"How young?"

"Too young."

"Do you mean like underage?"

"Not that young."

"And you don't approve."

"No!" Lark looked shocked. "Do you?"

Rachel had never given it much thought. She knew a few couples with age differences, and they seemed happy. Meanwhile, she and her ex-husband had been close in age, and look what had happened to them.

"Doesn't it bug you when movie heroes are paired with women half their age?" asked Lark.

"Maybe a little," Rachel admitted, and she couldn't deny, it had creeped her out when Saxby had given her the once-over at the nature center. Tucking her feet up in the seat, she watched Dorothy flirt across the aisle through the notch between the headrests. "Maybe turnabout is fair play," she said, jerking her head toward the front of the bus. "In this case, rather than a she's May and he's December romance, she's December and he's August."

Lark stuck her head out into the aisle, and then quickly pressed back against her seat. "He's October," she corrected, "which means we have nothing to worry about."

■ ■ ■ ■

Rachel must have dozed off, for the next thing she knew she was jolted awake as the bus lurched to a stop in front of the Sapelo Island Ferry building. Propelled by the salty sea air and a bevy of birders, she made her way onto the boat; a half hour later, she found herself standing at the rail scanning the Sapelo Island shoreline.

Waterfowl was scarce, the sign of an early spring, though several flocks of birds dotted the beach.

"Does everyone see the great black-backed gulls?" asked Saxby, pointing along the beach. "Beyond them is a flock of terns. On the far left, you'll see a gull-billed tern."

Rachel peered through her binoculars and panned the shore.

"Do you see it?" asked Lark.

"No." Rachel swept her glasses over the huddled terns, butts to the shoreline, their faces tipped to the wind. "Wait, does it have a black crown and a short black bill? Sort of light gray, with a white breast?"

"That's it."

"I count more than one."

"There are twenty four," affirmed Saxby. "Does everyone have them?"

A murmur passed through the crowd.

A few moments later, Dorothy picked up a whimbrel. The large gray-brown bird with its strong black head stripes poked its down-curved bill at the sand like a picky eater knocking peas aside with a fork.

Then the ferry docked, and Saxby gathered them around. "From here we go by hay wagon," he said. "Everyone sit in the middle and look to the outside. Whatever you do, hang on."

Dorothy grabbed Rachel's hand, pulling her up to the front to sit beside her and near Saxby. "Listen to him, dear," she said. "He knows his birds. When he points them out, you'll have a better chance of identifying them."

Rachel felt her feathers ruffle. The idea that Dorothy had announced she needed help annoyed her. Not that she didn't need help, mind you, but she had gotten better at birding in the past couple of years. She may have been a little raw the last time she had birded with Dorothy, but since then she had gone out birdwatching on a weekly basis with Kirk. Maybe she should state the obvious — that she was Dorothy's excuse for sitting near Saxby again.

The wagon lurched forward, and Rachel anchored herself on a hay bale as the truck jounced away from the beach. Passing the dunes, they moved into a new zone where wax myrtles — dwarfed and entangled with cat brier, pepper vine, Virginia creeper, and Muscatine grape — formed a shrubby thicket.

"We're going to make a few stops," announced Saxby. "This first habitat is called a shrub thicket. This will be the best location to see painted buntings, Acadian flycatchers, and yellow-rumped warblers."

"There's one," shouted an excited middle-aged woman.

"Keep your voice down!" ordered Saxby.

Startled, the woman's chin quivered.

Realizing his mistake, Saxby softened his expression, reached out, and patted her arm. "We need to use conversational voices when spreading the word," he said in a gentler tone. "Here we are close enough to the birds that we don't want to scare them. We want everyone to have a chance to see them."

"Acadian flycatcher," said Lark. "Passenger's side."

The woman flashed Saxby a watery smile, and turned to look.

"Painted bunting, two o'clock in the wax myrtles, driver's side," called out someone else.

"Butter-butt."

"Excuse me?" Rachel looked around to see who had said that, and spotted Dwayne, the bus driver, sitting two seats away.

"It's a local's nickname for the yellow-rumped warbler," he explained over his shoulder. "Little bird. Yellow rump."

"You're a birder?"

Now she sounded like Saxby. Dwayne had on all of the right garb, and he carried a pair of Zeiss binoculars.

"Of course you are," she said.

"Actually, I'm a swamp rat. My mother, my brother, and I run canoe tours in the Okefenokee Swamp."

"That's our Friday tour." She gestured between herself and Lark, Dorothy, and Cecilia.

"Sweet." He winked, and Rachel felt herself color.

He was flirting with her, not that he wasn't attractive in a rough sort of way. Tan, with tattoos that covered both of his forearms, his body looked made of hard work. Take away the small silver hoop earring that dangled from his left ear, and he could pass for a Marine.

"If you're a tour leader, why are you driving the bus?"

"It's the property of the Okefenokee

Swamp Tours. Evan came up a ride short, and I offered to help. It seemed like the neighborly thing to do. Besides," he winked again, "it gives me a chance to catch the view on Sapelo."

Rachel felt her face burn.

Dwayne turned back around, settled his baseball cap backward on his head, and pointed into the thicket. "There's another butter-butt."

Rachel turned her attention back to the birds, and to Saxby. He was the real target, and she needed to keep her eye on the ball.

All around them, people had set up spotting scopes. She had learned to use one in Elk Park, her first lesson being on that ill-fated day when Lark's business partner, Esther, was murdered. It had taken Kirk a while to get her to try scoping again, and now she was addicted. She had signed up for the digiscoping course on Thursday, and watched one man with particular interest.

"That's Chuck Knapp," said Saxby.

"Should I know him?" asked Rachel. He was a small man, and hairy, with a round bald spot on his pate. She couldn't recall ever having seen him before.

"He's a very famous filmmaker and wildlife photographer," said Saxby. "Everyone knows Knapp."

Not everyone. At the risk of coming off stupid, she asked, "What are some of his films?"

"His best known is the IMAX film *A Bird's-Eye View.*"

Rachel remembered seeing the movie, an hour-long feature from the perspective of a painted bunting as it escapes capture and migrates north from its wintering grounds. "Didn't it take an award for best documentary or best cinematography?"

"It was nominated for both," said Saxby, "but it didn't win either. Knapp tends to align himself with the wrong camp."

At that, Saxby stood and announced they were moving on. Rachel made a mental note to speak to Knapp later and ask about his upcoming projects.

Their next stop was the shrub forest. Here the trees — pine, yaupon holly, red cedar, red-bay, Hercules' club, and wax myrtles — had grown up, and there were more and more bird sightings.

"Prothonotary warbler," called out a man.

Rachel looked up, saw a golden flash, and then the bird lit high in the tree. *Weat, weat, weat, weat, weat.*

"Yellow warbler," said Saxby.

She swung her glasses to locate the bird, but spotted another. "Gray kingbird."

"Where?" demanded a chorus of voices.

"That's a rare sighting for here," said Saxby.

Rachel pointed to the bird perched on a utility wire running alongside the road. She only knew what it was from a trip she'd taken with Kirk to the Florida Keys. Whitish below, grayish above, with a heavier mask, a notched tail devoid of white, and a heavy black bill, it trilled *pe-teerr-it,* followed by a few other guttural and metallic sounds.

"By God, it is!" Saxby exclaimed, clapping her on the shoulder. "Well done."

Rachel kept her hands to herself.

CHAPTER 4

A half hour later, the group stopped for lunch in Hog Hammock, a dusty little town with small houses and an open-air market. The houses were brightly colored, and old women sat in rocking chairs on small covered porches. Tables had been set up in the shade, and younger women speaking a mixture of African and Elizabethan English served them a traditional meal of fish *perlo* — a one-pot rice dish made with a vegetable and/or meat, and traditionally seasoned with pork.

His plate filled to the brim, Saxby had made a beeline for the table where Rachel, Lark, Dorothy, and Cecilia sat under a spreading oak. Pleasantries were exchanged, and then Dorothy asked him what he knew about the people.

"They're part of the Geechee culture," he explained, "which dates back more than two hundred years. Of course, this community

67

only dates to 1950, when R. J. Reynolds instituted his land-consolidation plan." Saxby set down his fork, and used his hands to gesture. "There were black land holdings spread out all over the island," he said, carving the shape on a map in the air. "But Reynolds wanted to consolidate his holdings. He offered a trade, a plot of land and a house in Hog Hammock" — Saxby pointed to a spot on the fictional map — "for each black landowners' property." His hands swept over the imaginary island. "Needless to say, Reynolds came out ahead." Saxby picked up his fork. "The black landowners often ended up trading for less than they gave in the exchange."

"Then why did they trade?" asked Lark.

Saxby shrugged. "It's hard to say. The Geechee have a family-oriented culture. For example, it's customary for newlyweds to move into the husband's parent's home and live there until they can afford to build a home of their own. You can imagine how many multiple generational households there are. Plus, community grievances are settled in praise houses or churches." Saxby forked some more *perlo*. "Maybe it made sense to them to live closer together."

Or maybe they had felt some outside pressure to take the deal. Tired of listening to

Saxby, Rachel dabbed her mouth with her napkin, and excused herself. Crossing the soft grass, she browsed the stands the crafters had set up, and found herself drawn to the baskets of a beautiful dark-skinned woman in orange.

"*E be fanner,*" the woman explained, handing Rachel a paper. "De basket be used to throw de rice."

Rachel read the description.

A fanner is a traditional basket used to throw threshed rice into the air, allowing the wind to carry off the chaff. Originally made of bulrushes, today's baskets are made from sweetgrass taken from the dunes. Longleaf pine needles are used to make decorations, and palmetto leaves hold the coils together.

"Dat one be beautiful," said the woman, bestowing approval on the one Rachel held in her hands. "Dat one be fifty dollars."

"It's a good price," said Dwayne, materializing beside her. "It's an old art, and Trula's one of the best."

"Tank oon."

Dwayne nodded.

Rachel watched him walk away, before hemming and hawing over the price. She had no idea what a basket like this was worth. She only knew she wanted it. Finally, she dug out the money.

"Oona be happy," said Trula, wrapping the basket in plain paper, and slipping it inside a plastic bag. Then her expression changed, and she signaled for Rachel to move her head closer. "Come, lady."

Rachel leaned in, bumping her hip against the table.

Trula slipped Rachel the basket, but kept hold of one edge, whispering close to her ear. *"Oona mus tek cyear."*

"Excuse me?"

Trula's orange dress swirled about them in the breeze, her sleeve softly brushing Rachel's face. "Me sense *hudu.*"

"Hudu?"

"Bad luck," she whispered. *"Oona mus tek cyear."*

Rachel had to admit, the woman's premonition creeped her out. Still, they'd had good luck with the birds in the afternoon, and her spotting of the gray kingbird was voted the best catch of the day. Dusty and dirty, the busload of birders had arrived back at the Hyde Island Convention Center minutes before the kickoff festivities began, with no time to return to the hotel and change.

"I need to find a ladies' room," said Rachel, swatting dust from the legs of her pants.

"Okay," said Lark. "How about, we'll meet you at the bar?"

Dorothy, Cecilia, and Lark headed into the convention hall, while Rachel sniffed out a bathroom. A few minutes later, she checked out the damage in the bathroom mirror. Dust powdered her face, blotting out her freckles, and her hair feathered her white cap in a riot of curls. Wiping down her face with a paper towel, she stuffed her cap into her back pocket, and finger-combed her reddish hair into a French twist. Rolling her long-sleeved shirt into a belt, she cinched it around her waist, turned up the cuffs of her pants, and then waded back through the crowd. She found Lark standing at the bartender's station clutching a twenty-dollar bill in one hand.

"There you are," said Lark, her braid draping her shoulder like a thin, feather boa, tufts of blond hair sticking out at odd angles. "What do you want to drink?"

"A Pepsi."

"One Pepsi, two white wines, and a Coors light," ordered Lark, flashing the bartender a smile.

Rachel glanced around and sized up the

crowd. "I swear your numbers are off. There are nowhere near twelve hundred people in here. Five hundred, maybe."

"Not everyone shows up opening night," said Lark, snatching a handful of napkins off the counter and wafting them through the air. "A lot of these people are vendors and presenters."

"Along with a few hard-core birders," said Cecilia, coming up behind them. "Like us."

Like you. Rachel knew she didn't fit the category. At best, she could be called an advanced beginner birdwatcher. One who sometimes got lucky.

"It also gives anyone interested a chance to rub elbows with the stars," said Dorothy, panning the crowd.

"Mostly it gives potential buyers a chance to check out the stuff without pressure to buy." Lark handed Rachel her Pepsi, and nudged her into the aisle. "The vendors aren't allowed to ring up sales tonight."

As they wandered "The Nest," Rachel decided the event was a smart marketing plan. She had no doubts that most of these people would come back tomorrow to buy things. There was tremendous interest in the big-ticket items — the binoculars and scopes. Booth after booth carried brands from Bausch & Lomb to Zeiss. People waited in lines to focus demo scopes on the bird pictures taped high in the rafters, while more people pawed through display racks of clothing, bird feeders, books, artwork, sculptures, jewelry — anything imaginable that had a bird, insect, or wild animal on it.

"Check this out." Rachel pointed to a camouflaged exhibit spanning the south wall. A banner emblazoned with BEAU AND REGGIE'S BIRDS OF PREY stretched high above a twelve–tree stump display, camouflaged to depict a woodland scene. Various birds sat on the stumps, among them an American kestrel, a peregrine falcon, a prairie falcon, a bald eagle, a golden eagle, a great-horned owl, a northern harrier, and a red-tailed hawk. The birds eyed the crowd with a mixture of deference, disdain, and fear.

Lark swigged her beer and studied the peregrine. "I've seen this exhibit before. It's run by Beau and Reggie."

"Obviously," said Rachel. Lark's statement seemed redundant with the sign.

"They're considered the Siegfried and Roy of the raptor world."

"First it's the Indiana Jones of the birding world, then it's the Siegfried and Roy?"

Lark ignored her. "As I recall, they put on a pretty good show."

73

"They claim their birds are unfit for release," said Dorothy, punctuating her words with a sniff.

"Let me guess," said Rachel. "You don't believe them."

Dorothy shrugged. "I'll concede some of the birds may be injured, but wait until you see most of them fly. Beau and Reggie claim they were all donated from wildlife centers like the Raptor House."

Rachel felt her attitude shift at the mention of the Elk Park wildlife rehabilitation center. Once owned by her aunt Miriam and now run by the National Park Service, the Raptor House occasionally used birds for educational purposes, but most were rehabilitated into the wild. She couldn't imagine her aunt ever allowing them to be used in this type of display.

"Not only that," said Dorothy. "But the two of them are felons."

Cecilia, Lark, and Rachel turned to stare at her.

"I'm not kidding. I heard they both served time for trafficking wild birds. Parrots, to be exact."

"Oh my," said Cecilia. "Are you suggesting they have obtained *these* birds in a questionable manner?"

Lark scoffed at the whole idea. "Come on,

Dorothy. If they were felons, how would they get a license to put on this type of show?"

"That's a good question. Don't ask me. I'm just the messenger."

"Well, if they are felons," said Cecilia. "I think it's admirable they're now devoting their lives to educating people about the beauty of raptors."

Dorothy sniffed louder. "It's not like they're hurting for money."

Rachel didn't know what to think. She would have liked to see the show, but a plastic clock attached to the tree stump beneath the bald eagle indicated the next show wasn't scheduled to start for over an hour.

"We can come back," said Lark.

The women sauntered on, and for every stranger they encountered they met someone who either knew Dorothy, Lark, or Cecilia. Finally Rachel, her face muscles aching from smiling through all of the introductions, looked for a place to sit down.

"What do you say we perch over there for a few minutes?" She pointed toward the lunch area. The service counter was shuttered, but a long buffet table stacked with hors d'oeuvres cut a swath through a number of tables.

"Sure, why not?" Lark agreed.

Dorothy gripped Rachel's arm in a vise-like hold. "Wait! There's Guy."

Rachel's eyes flickered over the linen-draped tables, the metal chafing dishes, and the crowded groupings of diners until her eyes flitted over Saxby. He was seated at a table near the back with Paul Becker, Evan Kearns, Dwayne Carter, Patricia Anderson, the brunette from the parking lot, and four people Rachel couldn't identify.

Lark flipped back her braid. "For what it's worth, it looks like his table is full."

"Maybe, but there are open seats at the one beside it," said Cecilia, prying Rachel's arm loose of her sister's fingers. "Dorothy and I will go save them. Why don't you two go and get us some snacks?"

Before either of them could respond, Cecilia dragged Dorothy away. Lark rolled her eyes. Rachel reached for a dish.

"I feel like I'm back in high school," said Lark, scooping some spicy chicken wings onto her plate.

Rachel heaped hers with crab cakes. "I think it's kind of cute."

"That's because it gives you a way to help Kirk get his story."

Rachel stopped mid-pinch on a tongful of

pickled shrimp. Was Lark angry with her because Dorothy had a crush on Saxby?

"What are you saying? It's not like I've done anything to encourage her." And so what if she had? Rachel dropped the pickled shrimp on her plate. "Why are you so against Dorothy liking him, anyway?"

"She's a sixty-five-year-old spinster. He's a fiftysomething-year-old ladies' man." Lark stabbed some cocktail meatballs onto a toothpick, and then repeated the process. "I just don't want to see her get hurt, that's all."

"She's a big girl, Lark. Maybe she's just interested in having some fun." Rachel moved onto the tricolored tortellini skewers, her mouth watering at the savory smells of the buffet — Cajun spices mingled with oregano marinara and fresh-cooked fish.

"Right, but admit it. It makes your task easier." Lark scooped up some Cajun popcorn chicken and slopped it onto her plate.

Rachel jabbed at the honey-pecan chicken bites. "Okay, I admit it. So what?"

"It's not like Saxby's inaccessible," said Lark. "There are a lot more subtle ways for you to approach him than flinging our spinster friend at the target."

Rachel stopped mid-jab. "Tell me one thing I've done to encourage her?"

Lark moved onto the vegetarian offerings. "I'm just saying we need to discourage her, that's all."

"Then maybe you should be talking to Cecilia, not me."

Lark didn't say anything more, and they scooped their way through the rest of the chafing dishes in silence. Why had Lark taken such a dislike to Saxby? Rachel could understand her feeling protective of Dorothy, but Rachel couldn't see the harm in Dorothy's flirting with the man.

Trula's warning about *hudu* flitted through her brain as she rounded her plate with spinach-and-goat-cheese baguettes, toast points topped with Parmesan-artichoke soufflé, vegetarian pinwheel sandwiches, and crackers with a Southern pecan and Cheddar cheese ring filled with strawberry preserves. By the time she reached the end of the buffet tables she knew one thing — Southerners knew how to eat.

Plates heaping, the two of them wound their way through the tables toward the back. A couple from the Sapelo trip tried waving them over, but they forged ahead. By the time they arrived at where Dorothy and Cecilia were sitting, Saxby and the others had joined tables, and the sisters were ensconced in the group.

"Sit," said Saxby, waving them into the empty chairs. "Do you know everyone here?"

Rachel shook her head, while Lark set down the plates.

He started the introductions to his left, with the brunette from the parking lot. "This is Katie Anderson, the daughter of Patricia and Nevin Anderson, owners of the Hyde Island Club Hotel. Katie is a senior in high school this year."

And the spitting image of her mother, thought Rachel. She was maybe a few inches shorter, and her brown hair hung to her waist rather than at her ears, but the hazel eyes were the same and her attitude matched. With her blossoming figure overflowing her small camisole, and aware of her effect on the men at the table, she waved her hand like a princess. "Hello."

"Katie." Rachel waved with her fingers, and wondered what Patricia Anderson was thinking under her mask. She nodded curtly, while her husband, Nevin, barely acknowledged them. Instead, he nudged his wife in the ribs, and kept his rheumy eyes fastened on Katie.

"How could you let her go out wearing that outfit?" he muttered.

Saxby ignored the exhibit, and moved on

to the next man. "This is Victor Wolcott, president of the Hyde Island Authority."

Wolcott, a portly man of average height with a shock of gray hair and a bulbous nose, flashed a smile of perfectly straight, white teeth.

"The Hyde Island Authority?" said Rachel, accepting his handshake. "What's that?" It sounded like a transportation district.

"The Authority is the governing body of the island," explained Wolcott, "The whole island is owned by the State of Georgia. Simply put, the Authority acts as its agent."

That sounded official. "I think I remember reading something about that," said Rachel. "About how some millionaire deeded the land to a trust."

"In 1946," said Wolcott, with little prompting. "The island was owned by one man, Mr. Harry McKinlay. Finally tired of the upkeep and of running the Hyde Island Club, McKinlay retired and deeded the island to the State of Georgia. Whereby, the state of Georgia quickly passed a law requiring that 65 percent of Hyde Island remain in a natural state. The state then formed the Hyde Island Authority to oversee the land eligible for development. Among its other duties, the Authority negotiates long-term leases with business owners and residents, and approves any and all types of development. We —"

"Thank you, Victor," Saxby broke in. He gestured to the next in the circle. "I imagine you remember Evan Kearns, the conference coordinator."

Evan dipped his head.

"And Paul Becker."

Becker frowned.

"Beside Paul is his lovely wife, Sonja."

Sonja smiled. An exotic-looking woman with dark brown hair, she wore a fitted salmon-colored top, linen slacks, and her foot worked back and forth, kicking a stiletto slipper.

"And last, but not least, we have Fancy Carter and her two sons, Dwight and Dwayne. You remember Dwayne from the Sapelo trip. The Carter family owns and operates the Okefenokee Swamp Tours. They let us use their bus today."

Rachel nodded, pinching her lips together. Fancy Carter looked nothing like Rachel would have expected Dwayne's mother to look like. For starters, she didn't seem old enough to be the mother of an almost-thirtysomething-year-old man. Poured into her blue jean shorts, she wore her blonde hair Farrah Fawcett–style, while her hot-turquoise shirt exposed the upper half of a pair of double-D breasts.

Dwight, on the other hand, looked just like Dwayne. Tall, good-looking in a rough sort of way, with a buzz cut, a tattoo, and the "come hither" smile of a man who thinks he's all that with the ladies.

Becker cleared his throat. "Now that the introductions are over, can we rejoin our conversation?"

"I was listening, Paul," said Katie. She leaned forward suggestively and gave Becker her full attention.

Sonja glared.

Dwayne smiled.

Katie ignored them both.

"You were telling us about your great swamp adventure," she prodded, preening for full effect, then she softly started rubbing her belly.

Rachel wasn't sure what the gesture was for, or for whose benefit — Becker's or her mother's, perhaps? Rachel stole a glance at Sonja, who appeared to be on fire, and then in Patricia Anderson's direction. The woman seemed not to notice. Dwayne watched Katie intently.

"I made a trip out there two days ago," announced Becker. "I wanted to see for myself what was so special about that piece of land you're proposing to trade."

Rachel glanced at Lark, then at Dorothy and Cecilia.

The others looked just as confused as she felt.

It must have been evident none of them knew what the others were discussing because Nevin Anderson leaped to the rescue. "Patricia and I are trading ten thousand acres of swampland for eighty acres of land on Hyde Island adjacent to the golf course."

So that's what all the protest was about.

"Tentatively trading," corrected Wolcott. "The land swap is still pending the approval of the Authority."

"I take it you want to expand the golf course," said Lark.

Nevin Anderson smiled. "Sharp lady. You're the hotel owner, right?"

Lark nodded.

"It's a land swap I have been firmly against," announced Becker, reclaiming the spotlight. "The land adjacent to the golf course is prime habitat for the painted bunting, a species already endangered by Eastern Seaboard development. I see no reason to continue that trend on Hyde Island."

"Is there even land to be had?" asked Rachel. "Mr. Wolcott, didn't you say that 65 percent of the island has to remain in its natural state?"

Saxby grinned and stroked his beard. "Two sharp ladies."

"Call me Victor. And the answer to your questions are no and yes, but the Hyde Island Authority does have some wiggle room. Since it's the state that approached us to allow the trade, they are willing to let us increase the percentage of developable land by a fraction."

Becker cleared his throat. "After being out there, I can see why the state would want the swampland. It's certainly full of treasures." His mysterious tone drew everyone's attention. Dwayne and Dwight exchanged glances. "Suffice it to say, I had an interesting day."

"What kind of treasures are you talking about?" asked Dwight, craning forward to get a better look at Becker.

"He must mean he found some interesting birds," said Saxby.

"Indeed we did."

We?

Fancy chuckled. "What did you think, Dwight? That he meant he'd found one of your lost swamp treasures?"

Dwight glared at his mother, and Dwayne

bopped him on the backside of his head.

"Are there really lost swamp treasures?" asked Katie.

Fancy leaned forward, her shirt dropping open to reveal more cleavage. "Of course. Take my great-great-great-great-grandmother Aponi Carter, for example. Aponi was a Seminole princess, the daughter of a war chief. According to family history, her father was murdered during the Second Seminole War, and Aponi escaped into the northern swamp, bringing with her a family treasure. Some say it was a gift to her ancestors from a Spanish conquistador. Others say it's part of 'Caesar's Treasure,' the booty of a pirate who came ashore near her ancestral home."

The crowd had stilled. Even Katie had stopped rubbing her belly, and the neighboring tables were listening. Fancy played to the audience. "When she died, Aponi took the treasure to her grave. Her husband, honoring her wishes, constructed a burial mound deep in the swamp. On his deathbed, he confided in his sons the treasure's whereabouts, but due to his failing memory or the changing face of the swamp the treasure was never found." Fancy's voice dipped, like someone telling a ghost story around a campfire. Rachel felt shivers creep along her arms, and everyone else had leaned in close.

"You say there are other stories?" asked Lark.

"Hundreds," said Fancy, sitting back in her seat. Crossing her legs, she flipped her sandal with pink frosted toes. "The swamp has always been a favorite place for thieves and killers. Runaway slaves brought treasures off the plantations. Planes full of drugs have gone down and never been found. Hell, in the early 1900s, there was this bank robbery in Jacksonville where the robbers netted —"

"Excuse me," interrupted Becker. "But most of us are more interested in the birds."

Several people nodded their heads. Several others looked disappointed. Sonja rolled her eyes.

"That's why we're all here, after all," he continued.

Did Rachel detect a slur in his voice? Earlier he had banged down several drinks, and now he seemed agitated.

"You want to talk birds," said Saxby. "Let's talk birds. I went out to the Okefenokee Swamp myself, yesterday, and discovered a red-cockaded woodpecker on the nest."

"Which warrants some consideration

when deciding the trade," said Wolcott. "Certainly the red-cockaded woodpecker is more endangered by forestation practices than the painted bunting is by development on Hyde Island."

Rachel cocked her head. Based on the spin, Victor Wolcott must be pro-trade.

"I would agree with that," said Kearns, speaking up for the first time. "The swamp acreage is prime habitat for a number of species. And as the state has indicated they will purchase an additional fifty acres of dry land access for building a new welcome center and parking lot, the entire acerage will remain in a natural state. It's enough to make a difference. A big difference."

"How many groups of red-cockaded woodpeckers do you have in the Okefenokee National Wildlife Refuge?" asked Dorothy, looking at Saxby.

Lark leaned sideways, and whispered in Rachel's ear. "It takes anywhere from one hundred to five hundred acres of pine forest to support a group of red-cockaded woodpeckers."

"Twenty-nine at last count."

"But won't the swamp acreage stay in its natural state regardless of the trade?" asked Rachel. Knowing what she did about swampland, she found it hard to believe it was in great demand.

"That's one of the reasons we approached the Authority," said Nevin. "We've been contacted by a company with a special interest in the swamp acreage. The deal they're offering is even more lucrative for us than making the trade. If the Authority doesn't back us, we're going to sell."

He made it sound like a threat.

"What company?" asked Dwayne. "For what purpose?"

"I don't see where that's any of your business."

Dwayne's biceps bunched. "It sure as hell affects us."

Fancy reached out and patted his arm. "Let it go. He's bluffing. Besides, it doesn't endanger our deal. They'll still need dry land access."

The pieces dropped into place, along with the Carters' interest. No wonder Dwayne seemed worried.

"You're all missing the point," said Becker. "Either way, the land trade is detrimental. Either way, something precious is lost. It's been left up to us — you and me — to determine what's better sacrificed, and who — or what — will prevail."

CHAPTER 5

On that ominous note, Becker pushed away from the table. "We have an early start tomorrow. I'll see you all then," he said.

Katie was the next to leave, and Patricia Anderson quickly followed. Didn't she trust her daughter?

The Carters left next, then Evan Kearns departed.

Within moments, Rachel saw Lark give the high sign that it was time for them to depart.

"We should go, too," said Rachel. "We all have workshops the morning." She nudged Cecilia, who nudged Dorothy, and the four of them stood to go.

"Mind if I tag along?" asked Saxby. He slid back his chair and stood. "Perhaps I can even buy you ladies a nightcap?"

Cecilia raised an eyebrow at her sister. "Oh my."

Dorothy turned beet red.

Lark glared.

"Why not?" said Rachel, covering an awkward silence. Heck, it might be her last opportunity to get the skinny on Saxby. "It's apt to be a little crowded, but I think we have room for one more in the car."

Now Lark scowled. Rachel didn't want to know what she was thinking.

With Saxby settled into the backseat between Cecilia and Dorothy, Lark drove and Rachel rode shotgun. Lark rolled down the windows, which discouraged conversation, so Rachel leaned her head against the backrest and absorbed the hum of the cicadas, breathing in the sweet scent of magnolias and letting the soft breeze ruffle her hair.

The protestors were out in force, and Rachel could hear them before she could see them. "No Land Swap! No Land Swap!" She felt a pang of sympathy for their cause. The painted buntings were beautiful birds, and it seemed a shame to wipe out their nesting area for nine more holes of golf. Death shoots a birdie on the eighteenth hole.

She smiled at their leader, and the man smiled back. Today he wore a white T-shirt with the image of a golf green circled and slashed, and multiple strands of love beads.

Once they were headed up the drive of the Hyde Island Club Hotel, Cecilia spoke up. "I'm exhausted. I think I'll bow out and head straight up to bed. Anyone care to join me?"

She plucked at Rachel's sleeve, and Rachel batted her hand away. What she had to say wouldn't make Cecilia happy. "I could go for a coffee and Baileys."

Regardless of how ridiculous she considered Lark's attitude toward Saxby, if Lark thought Dorothy needed chaperoning far be it from Rachel to abandon ship.

Lark thawed a degree. "Sounds good to me."

It ended up being the five of them. Cecilia had grudgingly changed her mind, and traipsed after them into a cozy bar off the dining room. Inside, fishnets loaded with stuffed sea bass and conch shells decorated the walls, candles under glass flickered from bare-top tables, and a bluegrass band picked "Li'l Georgia Rose" from a CD player behind the bar.

The place was practically empty. One well-lubricated gentleman mumbled into his drink at a corner bar stool, and several couples spooned at moonlight-draped tables near the windows. One extra-large table sat open near the crackling wood fire, and

Saxby guided Dorothy into a chair. He claimed the seat beside her, and Cecilia the seat beside him. Lark plunked down opposite, leaving Rachel a seat next to the screened-in window.

Once they were situated, conversation stalled. Rachel peered out and drank in the Georgia night. Palm trees rustled in the sweet-smelling breeze. Moonlight dappled the water. And farther out, a large cruise ship floated at the edge of the horizon where the deep blue of the sea met the slate blue–black of the sky.

"Ten thousand acres of swampland for eighty prime acres of golf course," Rachel mused. "Now that sounds like a sweet deal."

"You've never been there, have you?" Saxby asked.

"The swamp? No," she admitted. "We're going on Friday. It makes me think of that old joke. You know the one: 'I have some swampland I'll sell you.' "

"It's a unique habitat, and quite a resource," said Saxby, without cracking a smile. He was interrupted by a waitress in a crisp white shirt and denim skirt, who took their drink orders. When she left, Saxby resumed the conversation with a monologue on birding coastal Georgia.

"The state has a wide variety of habitats

and more than three hundred bird species," he droned. "We've just developed a coastal birding trail running all the way from Fort Pulaski National Monument to the Okefenokee National Wildlife Refuge."

Rachel watched the big ship cruise out of sight while Saxby gave detailed descriptions of the eighteen birding sights. His ability to breathe in mid-sentence shut off any opportunity for someone to break in, and it unnerved her. She began to wonder if anyone could ever succeed at getting a word in edgewise.

"More coffee?" asked the waitress, talking over the top of him, brandishing a fresh pot of coffee.

Saxby held up his cup. "The only problem is they failed to include Hyde Island on the list. It has some of the best birding in the state, yet they neglected to list it as a featured stop." He breathed, and said, "Thank you."

Rachel took advantage of the lull.

"So, Guy, tell us what comes next for you?" she asked, hoping that in his talkative mood he'd spill the beans and she'd have something to report to Kirk.

"Subtle," murmured Lark.

Rachel shot her a glare.

Saxby narrowed his eyes, and bounced a

glance between them. "I'm sorry, did I miss something?"

Rachel pasted on a smile and shook her head.

Saxby looked bemused. Tiny crows' feet crinkled at the corners of his eyes and a crease furrowed his brow.

Rachel bit her lip and waited for his answer.

Finally, after rubbing his jaw between thumb and forefinger, he twirled the spoon in his coffee and said, "I'm not sure I follow."

Rachel didn't buy the act. "Your adventures are legendary. Take your last one. Weren't you in Australia?"

"Ah." His eyes lit up. "You read about that?"

It was a rhetorical question, so she didn't answer.

"We didn't get the bird."

"I read that, too."

"What a shame," said Lark. Her voice dripped as much sarcasm as the live oak next to the patio dripped Spanish moss. Rachel kicked her under the table.

"Surely you have something else in the works," said Rachel.

Saxby cupped his hands around the ends of the armrests like he meant to get up, but instead settled back in his chair. "I'll admit, I have a plan."

Here it comes. Rachel scooted her chair closer.

"Unfortunately, you'll have to wait." He grinned and turned his palms up. "I was set to unveil it on Saturday, but of course that's been changed."

"Why not tell us now? We can keep a secret." Rachel hadn't come this far just to give up.

Dorothy shot Rachel a glare, and placed her hand on Saxby's sleeve. "She's joking. Why not unveil it on Friday night?"

Saxby patted Dorothy's hand. "Would that I could. Unfortunately, it's out of my hands. It all depends on whether or not the others can be ready in time."

"What others?" pressed Rachel.

Saxby clucked at her from the corner of his mouth. "I'm afraid you'll have to wait just like everyone else."

"Whatever it is, it sounds intriguing," said Dorothy.

Rachel tensed. Dorothy, normally quick-witted and sharp-tongued, had become positively cloying. *This wasn't good.*

"Then tell us something you *can* talk about," said Lark, who seemed equally agitated by Dorothy's manner. "Like, explain what's really going on between you and Paul Becker? He seemed pretty intent on putting you in your place."

Dorothy's face blanched. "Lark!"

"No, it's okay," said Saxby, reaching for his coffee. He took a quick sip, then set it down and traced his finger along the rim of the mug. "Paul Becker used to be my teacher's aide at the University of Georgia. When he left academia, I stayed. Now he's back, and he and I are colleagues again." Saxby looked up and met Lark's gaze "What can I say? I have a better office."

The evening wound down quickly after that. Everyone was scheduled to attend early-morning workshops, so after a little more banter, they bid Saxby goodnight. Dorothy had followed Cecilia into their room and had banged the door sharply. The adjacent room door remained latched.

"I'm going to shower," said Lark.

While she was in the bathroom, Rachel tried calling Kirk.

"You've reached Udall. I can't come to the phone right now . . ."

She listened through the message, allowing his rich baritone to embrace her, then hung up before the beep. He was, after all, in Sri Lanka. She had no idea what the time difference was, but if she wanted to connect with him her best bet was through e-mail.

Setting her laptop up on the desk, she plugged it into the Ethernet and checked her messages. There were at least twenty from her office. She answered the important ones, then typed out a message to Kirk.

You'll never guess who I had drinks with tonight. Guy Saxby! He admits he has a new project, but refused to give any details. I'll keep working on him. He seems enamored with Dorothy Mac-Bean.

She paused, and then added:

Wish you were here. Rachel

Hitting the Send button, she shut down the laptop and stretched out on the bed, listening to the beat of the shower. She allowed her mind to drift, and conjured an image of Kirk. In khaki shorts and Hawaiian shirt, he stood surrounded by the devastation of the tsunami, staring at the surf. She thought she heard him wondering how in the heck he could focus on the birds.

"Rise and shine."

Rachel's eyes fluttered open. What time was it?

Dorothy stood over her, wearing a light pink shirt with a band of yellow warblers flitting across the chest. Exaggerated by the humidity, her hair curled tightly around her face like a clown's wig, and accentuated her pale gray eyes. "We are going to be late."

"For what?" Rachel realized she was sprawled under the comforter wearing the same clothes she'd had on yesterday. *Shoot.* She must have fallen asleep. "What time is it?"

"Seven o'clock. And you and I are scheduled for the warbler identification class this morning at eight, remember?"

Rachel kicked off the blanket. "Where are Lark and Cecilia?"

"At breakfast. They don't have to be there until nine. Now get moving!"

Rachel showered and dressed in record time. Toweling her hair dry, she threw on a pair of pants, a T-shirt, socks, tennis shoes, and grabbed a long-sleeved shirt from the dresser. Her backpack still held all the necessities — binoculars, field guide, sunscreen, tissues, and Chapstick.

"Are you ready?" Dorothy called out, while Rachel was brushing her teeth.

"Two minutes," she answered. It took her that long to French braid her hair. "Done, with a half hour to spare."

"Good. Let's go."

They pounded downstairs to the foyer, where a coffee kiosk beckoned. The scent of dark French roast coffee and warm Danishes mingled in the air. Rachel started toward the display, and Dorothy grabbed her arm.

"You can get coffee at the convention center."

"Not good coffee." Rachel glanced at her watch and stood her ground. "We have time."

Dorothy looked down at her feet, and Rachel's morning fog lifted.

"I get it," she said. "You want to catch Guy Saxby before classes begin."

Dorothy snapped her head up. "I don't know what you're talking about."

"Admit it. You have a crush on him."

"I'm sixty-five. I am too old to have a crush on anyone, especially someone ten years my junior."

"You can't fool me. Admit it. He is sort of sexy."

"Rachel!" Dorothy tried acting shocked, then broke down and giggled. "Okay, I'll admit, he makes me think of 007." Growing serious, her eyes darted toward the dining room entrance. "Now, if it's okay with you, I'd like to get over there before Lark and

Cecilia catch on."

That made sense. "But we only have one car."

"I left a note for Cec saying we took a cab."

Was she an accomplice or a dupe, Rachel wondered. Either way, she abandoned the idea of coffee and followed Dorothy outside. A wave to the protestors and a three-dollar cab ride landed them in front of the convention center five minutes later, with twenty minutes to spare.

With no field trips scheduled, the place pulsed with life. Birders mingled in the entryway, coffee cups in hand, and Rachel felt jealous.

"Did you make plans to meet somewhere?" she asked, figuring that if Dorothy hadn't there was no way she would find him in this crowd.

"We're meeting up by the Leica display."

The two of them pushed their way across the lobby to the vendors' area, where they were promptly stopped by a beefy security guard.

"No one's allowed into the Nest until eleven o'clock," he drawled. Laying on the Southern charm, he flashed a bright white smile and cocked his head.

"But I'm supposed to meet someone inside."

"No one's allowed," he repeated, crossing his arms and using his elbow-to-elbow girth to block the doorway.

"Thanks," said Rachel, pulling Dorothy aside.

Dorothy started to protest.

Rachel reasoned with her. "If we can't get in, he can't either. He did say nobody gets in."

"But the vendors can," said Dorothy. "And I'll bet the presenters can, too."

Rachel pondered, weighing the risks, and then said, "I know another way."

"How?"

"Follow me, and try to act natural." She guessed she had now assumed the mantle of accomplice. Flashing the security guard a smile, she led Dorothy past another set of locked double doors to a hallway on the right. "The public bathrooms are down this way, and there's another entrance to the vendors' area," she said in a hushed voice. "That entrance can't be locked off. Let's hope it's not guarded."

The entrance to the bathroom was halfway down the hall. Rachel glanced around to make sure no one had followed them, then scurried past the doorway to the ladies' room. At the end of the hallway, a moveable wall blocked the entry to the vendor's area.

"Keep your eyes open," said Rachel, leaning her shoulder into the wall. It moved slightly, but took a second shove before sliding back far enough for Rachel to slip through. "The coast is clear," she whispered.

Dorothy slipped through behind her. "Push it back into place," she whispered back, excitement tingeing her voice. "In case someone comes. I wonder if Guy was able to get in."

"Do you want me to wait here?" asked Rachel.

"No," said Dorothy, gripping her arm. "I want you to come with me."

The room was large, with no lights on and only a panel of windows along the back wall. In the twilight the cloth-draped displays looked like ghosts grouped for a photo shot. The two of them circled the lunch area, and headed toward the far wall. To the best of Rachel's recollection, the Leica booth was near the windows, across from Beau and Reggie's Birds of Prey display.

"Guy?" Dorothy called out using a stage whisper.

Rachel thought she heard a rustle. Was it was Saxby or one of Beau and Reggie's birds? She braced for a scare.

"Guy?" Dorothy called out again.

There was another rustle, followed this time by what sounded like a struggle. Two angry voices conferred, but Rachel couldn't make out the words.

Dorothy stopped dead in her tracks.

"Don't stop now," said Rachel. She was curious about the commotion. It sounded like two people wrestling in the next aisle.

Dorothy may as well have been paralyzed. She stood stock-still, her hands clenched at her sides, her face a ghostly shade of white. Was she afraid she'd find Saxby in some sort of tryst? Not likely, based on the tone of the voices.

Rachel gripped her shoulders. "Here, I'll take a look," she whispered. "It's probably Beau and Reggie working with the birds. I'll bet Guy's not even here yet."

Moving past Dorothy, Rachel tiptoed forward. She wished she could make out the words. She only caught snatches. She heard the word *swamp,* the word *trade,* and then *put that away.* Someone cursed, then her shoulder brushed against a rack of clothes at the end of the aisle, and all she could hear was the clanging of hangers banging against each other.

She froze.

The clanging subsided, but the room had

grown deathly still.

"No!"

Guy Saxby?

A sharp retort shattered the silence, followed by a splintering of glass.

She heard another sharp retort, and dropped to her knees. It sounded like gunfire.

CHAPTER 6

Rachel pulled Dorothy down beside her. A third shot rang out, then a fourth. *Who the hell was shooting?*

Pressing her face against the cold linoleum, Rachel searched the floor for a pair of feet, a flash of pant leg, anything that might signal where the shooter was standing.

Her heart pounded. Her breath came in quick, short gasps.

Calm down, Wilder. It isn't going to help to panic.

She held her fingers to her lips, as much to quell her own hard breathing as to keep Dorothy quiet. Shock had done a good job up until now, but the older woman's face looked pinched, with a side of tears imminent.

Think, Wilder!

What about the security guard? He had been standing outside the main doors not ten minutes ago. He had to have heard the shots. That meant someone would be in here soon to investigate, and they'd be discovered.

Holding Dorothy's hands in a viselike grip, Rachel listened for the sounds of a rescue.

Nothing. But then, she hadn't heard any sound for at least a minute, except for the pounding of her heart.

Rachel released Dorothy's hands and eased herself onto her elbows. She listened hard. There was a creak behind her. It came from the opposite side of the room. Was someone sneaking out the same way she and Dorothy had come in?

Climbing onto her hands and knees, Rachel glanced behind her, gesturing for Dorothy to stay on the floor. While she might be able to go slinking around on all fours, she figured that would be too much for Dorothy.

Instead of staying put, Dorothy crawled forward and lifted the table skirt, wearing an expression of shock. "It's him!" she whispered, her voice rising in panic.

"Who? Saxby?"

"He . . . he's on the floor. I can see his feet."

Rachel crouched down and looked under the table. In the gap between the cloth coverings and the floor poked a sneaker-shod foot, flat on the ground, but pointing right toward them from the next aisle.

"Stay here," Rachel whispered.

She moved slowly to the end of the row, staying low and listening. A squeak behind her made her start.

"You're not leaving me behind," said Dorothy. She, too, was crouched low.

Rachel rounded the table at the end of the aisle, and stopped abruptly. In the dim light she could see a man stretched out on the floor. Aside from the sneakers, he wore standard birding attire — shorts and a vented shirt. His upper torso and face were hidden under a gray cloth, but there was no concealing the hole in his back, or the blood puddled on the gray carpet.

"Guy!" Dorothy called out, scrambling to her feet and starting forward. Rachel reached up and pulled her down.

"Stay low, Dorothy. We don't know where the shooter is."

"Probably long gone," insisted Dorothy. "And he needs help."

Rachel shook her head. *He's beyond help.* "We need to get the security guard."

"I can't just leave a person in need. There has to be something we can do."

She was right. Saxby — at least, Rachel

assumed it was Saxby — didn't appear to be breathing, but the light was dim and his breathing could be shallow. She inched forward. She had done this before, checking a body for a pulse. She had hoped never to have to do it again.

Creeping to within inches of the body, she balked at touching his arm. It was startlingly warm. Her fingers probed his wrist, but she couldn't detect a beat.

"We're not experts," she said to Dorothy, whose face shone pale in the gloom. "We need to get help."

As if in response, Rachel heard a sudden rush of noise. The doors were flung open and all the noise from the hall poured inside, filling the silence.

"And to think that only last night —" Dorothy sniffled.

The burly security guard appeared, and Rachel leapt to her feet.

A frown creased his brow. "I told you, nobody is allowed in here."

Rachel pointed to the ground. "We need an ambulance! Now! A man's been shot!"

Things happened quickly after that. The security guard had repeated Rachel's futile quest for a pulse, then used his radio to call in the emergency. By then, Dorothy had crept forward and kneeled beside the body.

"It's not —"

"At all cool that you're in here," supplied the security guard. He gripped Rachel's arm with one hand, and Dorothy's arm with the other. "It don't matter if he's your friend, dead is dead. You're contaminating a crime scene." He herded everyone who had followed him in back out of the Nest, and then delivered Rachel and Dorothy into the hands of the police.

After that, things slowed down. The police taped off the entrance past the bathroom, barricaded the doors into the Nest, sequestered Dorothy somewhere, and put Rachel in a small, cold conference room where she sat for an interminable time.

Too bad she hadn't gotten that coffee. Too bad they hadn't been five minutes later. But it was Dorothy she felt most sorry for. At least Cecelia had gotten her three-day honeymoon. Dorothy had barely begun to flirt.

Eventually, a skinny black detective entered the conference room and made Rachel tell her story. Then he asked a few questions.

"What made you think there had been a scuffle?"

"Because it sounded like two people were

fighting. Men, by the sound of their voices. I only picked up snatches of their conversation." She told him the words.

"How many shots were fired?"

"Three, no four, I think."

And then he had her go over it again.

"Where are you from?"

"New York City."

"What do you do there?"

"I work in graphic production."

"How long have you known Dorothy Mac-Bean?"

"Nearly three years." She hoped she wouldn't have to tell him that she had found a dead body then, too.

"Who were you meeting in the vendors' area?"

"Guy Saxby," said Rachel. "I can't believe he's dead." She wanted to lie down.

"Did you talk to him?"

"No." She wanted to ask if she was a suspect, but that seemed like it might fall into the category of stupid question.

"And you didn't see anyone else?"

"No."

"Is there anything else you remember? Anything you haven't told me?"

"No."

At last the detective leaned forward. "All right, Ms. Wilder. Thank you for your cooperation. You're free to go."

Rachel stood up, feeling lightheaded. "Aren't you going to tell me not to leave town, or something?"

"You're staying until what . . . Sunday? We'll talk before then. But it would be best if you didn't talk to anyone about any of this. We don't need you muddying up the waters."

Speaking of talking with someone.

"Can you tell me where my friend is?" she asked.

"The older lady?"

Rachel nodded.

"Check with the sentry."

Rachel stepped out into the hall and blinked. A bank of windows let in the sunlight. The conference room was gloomy by comparison. So much for the famous bright lights of the interrogation room.

She found the guard outside the doorway, but he couldn't tell her a thing.

Stay on task, Wilder. She had to find Dorothy. Surely they weren't still asking her questions.

Rachel walked the hallway of the conference center without a clear plan. Out of nowhere, the Geechee woman's prediction rang again in her head. *"Oona mus tek cyear."* Take care.

111

Find Dorothy. If the police were through talking with her, she might have headed back to the hotel. Or maybe not. She might have waited for Rachel. Even really upset, Dorothy was tough.

Coffee, maybe that would help her think. Rachel looked for an Exit sign, getting a vision of herself walking through the corridors of the conference center forever. She turned the corner, and her stomach growled. She hadn't had any breakfast or lunch, either. Glancing at her watch, she was stunned to find out it was only 10:45 a.m.

Rachel hadn't paid much attention as the policeman had guided her through the conference center, but it soon became clear that the room where she'd been interrogated was in the Lucy Bell wing. In her search for an exit, she passed groups of stylishly dressed conferees who gave her brief, pitying looks. Apparently she was in need of a makeover, or maybe at this point it was hopeless.

She turned another corner and, to her amazement, there stood Dorothy and a tall man.

"Dorothy!" she said, then realized who she was standing beside. "Guy Saxby!"

"In the flesh," he said again, but more

somberly than the first time.

"I'm okay, dear," Dorothy said. "But Guy is being taken downtown." She gestured haphazardly with her hands. "Wherever that is."

"It's nothing," Saxby said.

"Then who . . . ?"

"Becker," Dorothy answered grimly.

Saxby nodded, just as the wiry black deputy who had interrogated Rachel came out of a doorway carrying a hot cup. "Ready to roll?" he asked Saxby.

Guy shrugged in Dorothy's direction. "I'll see you later," he said. "This shouldn't take long, really."

Dorothy grabbed Rachel's arm as the three men walked away. "You looked like you'd seen a ghost!"

"Well, I thought it was Guy lying in there," Rachel said. "Didn't you?"

"At first. Only because I was meeting him," Dorothy said. "When I knelt beside the body, I saw it was Becker, but by then the security guard had arrived and separated us."

"The cops didn't tell me anything," said Rachel. "That's why, when I saw him —"

"It was obvious what you thought."

"How did he find you?"

"Once he heard I was being questioned,

he insisted on seeing me. The guard allowed it. I mean, he isn't a suspect or anything."

"We're all suspects, Dorothy."

"Rubbish. I don't believe that."

Something didn't make sense. Realizing they were drawing attention standing in the middle of the hallway, Rachel grabbed Dorothy's arm and steered her toward the Hyde Island Birding and Nature Festival side. "Let's go back to the hotel. We can leave a message for Lark and Cecilia on the message board."

At the entrance to the Nest, Rachel was surprised to find the festival in full swing. Both double doors were propped open, and the crowd perused the booths like nothing had happened. Peeking inside, Rachel could see that the crime scene had been cordoned off with makeshift walls, but nearly half of the vendors were open for business.

Rachel scribbled a note for Lark, thumbtacked it to the message board, and then hailed a cab. She and Dorothy didn't talk on the way to the hotel, and neither of them acknowledged the protestors. Rachel freshened up while they waited for room service to deliver them lunch. Now, seated at the small breakfast table in her room with the food barely touched, she couldn't help but wonder why Saxby had left the Nest without them.

"Doesn't it seem odd that he would just leave us in there with someone shooting a gun? He had to have heard you call out."

Dorothy looked shocked. "He wasn't even in there. He said the guard wouldn't let him through."

Then who had she heard sneaking away?

Rachel sipped her coffee, setting it down with a bang. "Think back, Dorothy. The scuffle came before the shot, before the glass shattered. I'll bet the shot came from outside."

Dorothy face paled. "That means we fingered Guy by telling the police we were there to meet him. We dropped the dime on him. We flushed him out."

"If he didn't do it," Rachel mused.

"Of course he didn't do it!" Dorothy's eyes flashed. "Any more than we did!"

Rachel wasn't so sure. Saxby was territorial, if that was a reason to kill Becker. Still, she reassured Dorothy. "If he's telling the truth, the guard at the doors will remember turning him away, just like he did us."

"But we got inside. They'll just say he entered the same way we did." Dorothy crumbled a piece of toast into a mini sand dune on her plate. "We're going to have to help clear him." She dusted her hands together. "We can help the police."

"How?"

"By giving them a list of suspects."

"Like who?" asked Rachel. "We don't know who might want Becker dead."

"How about those who are for the land swap?" said Dorothy. "Becker was against it."

"That gives us the Andersons. They're the only ones we really know are pro-trade."

"It's a start," said Dorothy. "Becker said he had found a 'treasure,' remember. What if he was about to reveal something that would stop the deal?"

"Then the Andersons would be out a golf course." Rachel reached for her coffee again. "And how bad could that be? They already have a nine-hole course. If they don't get to expand, it won't be the end of the world." Rachel took a sip, then cradled her coffee against her chest. "I'll admit, eighty acres of prime land next to the hotel would be an improvement over ten thousand acres of swampland, but it's not worth killing anyone over. And either way, they make out."

"Then suppose what he discovered impacts the Carters? Those boys seemed pretty upset when Becker mentioned finding

116

something out there."

"But Fancy didn't seem worried. The same goes for Dwight and Dwayne. Either the state wants their land, or the developers do. Either way, they come out ahead. It's win-win."

"Unless the state would no longer need access," said Dorothy.

"In which case, they wouldn't want the trade to happen and we're back to the Andersons as our only suspects." Rachel tapped her finger against her mug. "Doesn't it seem odd that both Guy Saxby and Paul Becker seemed to have big revelations on tap?"

"What are you suggesting?" asked Dorothy. "Are you thinking it was the same revelation? It couldn't be."

"It might be related," said Rachel. "Remember what a big deal they made about which one of them got the Saturday keynote slot. They both wanted it."

"And Guy gave the slot to Becker, even though it cost him." Dorothy drew herself up. "Let's get one thing straight, missy. Guy Saxby is not a killer. I'm a good judge of character. Besides, even if he was a murderer, he wouldn't kill somebody over a better keynote slot. He said himself that he hoped to be able to unveil his next big adventure on Friday."

Rachel took a sip of her drink. "I wonder if Guy will tell us what he's up to, reveal his big secret, now that all this has happened."

Dorothy narrowed her eyes. "If you're looking to give your boyfriend some front-page news, isn't the murder of Paul Becker enough?"

The truth hit home. Rachel's cheeks started to heat, and then guilt set in. Her friend was really worried about this man. Setting down her cup, she reached for Dorothy's hand. "I'm sorry. So what could Becker have discovered that could possibly be big enough to kill him over?"

Neither of them could think of a thing.

CHAPTER 7

Before they could take up the subject again, the hotel room door swung open and Lark and Cecilia burst into the room.

"With all the excitement over there, how could you leave?" The sweat gleaming on Lark's forehead was the only indication she had run up the stairs. "Or maybe you didn't hear. Somebody killed Becker."

Rachel nodded. "We know."

"We found him," announced Dorothy.

Lark and Cecilia gasped.

Cecilia hurried over and fluttered around her sister. "Oh my, oh, Dot."

"Are you two okay?" asked Lark.

"We're fine," said Dorothy, batting Cecilia away. "But the cops have Guy. They took him downtown and everything."

Cecilia pulled up a chair and patted her sister's thigh. "That's what everyone was saying, so when we couldn't find you, of course we thought . . ." She let her sentence dangle, but Dorothy jumped to the bait.

"You thought they had dragged us off, too?"

"Of course not." Cecilia sounded indignant. "We thought you might have gone with him."

That seemed to mollify Dorothy. "They did question us. I talked with a very nice young man. I suppose he was the good cop. I guess Rachel got the bad cop. She got the same one who dragged Guy away."

"Guy went willingly, and the detective, he was okay," said Rachel. "He kept asking me the same questions over and over, but that's his job. He was nice about it."

"Give us details," said Lark. "We want to hear everything that happened."

With the detective's admonition to keep quiet playing in her head, Rachel gave her rendition of the story, then Dorothy gave hers.

"It fits," said Lark. "The buzz at the festival is that Saxby is the main suspect."

"Rubbish." Dorothy looked pointedly at each of them. "He's innocent, and we plan to prove it."

"How?" asked Cecilia. It was like hearing an echo of herself, thought Rachel.

"Why?" asked Lark.

"Because I know he's innocent, and the

police think he's guilty because of us. Besides, it's not like we haven't solved a murder before."

"No, we've solved three," said Cecilia.

"Or two, in my case," said Rachel. She had been in Elk Park for the murder of Esther Mills, Lark's late partner in the coffee company, and for the murder of the reporter from *Birds of a Feather* magazine, who was doing the exposé on her aunt's late husband. That one had struck too close to home.

"So far we have the Andersons on our list," said Dorothy. "Can you think of anyone else who might want Becker dead?"

"What about his wife?" asked Cecilia.

Dorothy frowned. "Why would she want to kill him?"

"Because most murders are crimes of passion, committed by someone close to the victim," Cecilia replied. "Usually someone from the immediate family."

She'd been watching too much *CSI*.

"I knew that," said Dorothy.

"Did you ever want to kill Roger?" asked Lark.

Rachel looked up sharply. She met Lark's stare and had to admit the thought had crossed her mind. "Before or after the divorce?"

They all laughed at her joke, but Rachel

wasn't laughing too hard.

"I need to get out of here," she said, rising to her feet. "Anyone up for a walk on the beach?"

"I'll go," said Lark.

Cecilia looked at Dorothy, who hedged. "If you don't mind, I'd like to wait here."

Cecilia stayed behind with Dorothy. Lark and Rachel took the car. Lark drove, honking and waving merrily at the protestors as they sped out the gate. The dark-haired hippie type smiled and waved back.

Lark parked the car at the soccer fields, at the north end of south beach, and they walked the boardwalk, their binoculars looped loosely around their necks. Exiting the forest, they found themselves over the dunes. Carolina willows, smartweed, and a large clump of Hercules' club lined the boardwalk. The farther they walked the shorter the oaks, buckthorn, and other shrub-forest trees became, while the wax myrtles increased in numbers. Then they were across the beach meadows and onto the beach.

Birds flitted in the bushes, hidden from sight except for brief flashes of color, but Rachel didn't know her birdsongs well enough to identify any of them. Besides, she wanted to be on the beach. Pushing on, they crossed the meadows, reached the shore, and headed off to the southwest, their feet churning the sand. Up ahead someone allowed their dog off leash, and it bolted into the dunes.

Lark snorted. "We should report them."

"If we get close enough we can yell at them." That might relieve some of the tension building in her neck and shoulders. Dogs and people were the dunes' worst enemies. High seas and heavy winds did enough damage. Not only that, but the dog chased the birds off the beach, giving Lark and Rachel little chance of seeing anything.

They ambled along, enjoying the sun and air, until Rachel picked up some movement in the sand. She stopped. A small, sandy-brown bird with white underparts, orange legs, an orange bill with a black tip and a black neckband harvested shells along the edge of the dunes. "Is that a piping plover?"

Lark raised her binoculars. "It sure is. Good spotting."

They watched it for a few moments, then passed by near the water's edge to afford the bird plenty of room.

The sighting spurred them to birdwatch, and they had soon added two handfuls of other species to their list. Sanderlings, a ruddy turnstone, a spotted sandpiper, laughing gulls, ring-billed gulls, and herring gulls came first. Then a flock of brown pelicans buzzed the surf, like B-52 bombers on a surveillance run, and a flock of black skimmers passed by, their white bellies skimming the surface of the sea. A grouping of terns and gulls clustered at the surf's edge turned up three new species. The Caspian terns were the largest, their thick orange bills, black crowns, and black legs distinctive against the white sand. Then came the royal terns, with their white caps and yellow bills. Tucked in among the others Rachel spotted a sandwich tern, its black beak and black crown making it stand out among the giants.

By then they had walked nearly to the tip of the south beach. There, picnickers dotted the sand, while a group of wood storks and egrets fished the surf. Farther out, four men seined for shrimp.

"Ready to turn around?" asked Lark.

Rachael lifted her face to the sun, relished the feel of salt spray on her face, and rolled her shoulders. "Ready."

The hike in and out had taken nearly two hours. They dallied on the boardwalk, treated to the antics of a painted bunting and his ladies along the rail, and then they made a quick stop at the conference center to see what — if anything — had been altered on the program. A stack of notices announced a change of keynote speaker for Saturday night, and it wasn't Guy Saxby. Instead, the committee had chosen the film-maker Chuck Knapp.

Lark snorted. "I'll bet that frosts Saxby. That makes him last choice." She seemed almost gleeful.

"I wonder whose decision it was," said Rachel. She presumed Evan Kearns. As much as Saxby hadn't liked the idea of switching keynote slots with Becker, Kearns had quickly jumped on the idea.

Back at the hotel, Rachel knocked on the adjoining door and handed a copy of the notice to each of the sisters.

"I see they're doing a tribute to Becker," said Cecilia. "That's nice."

Dorothy jabbed her finger at the note about Saturday night. "I imagine 'the committee,'" she intoned sarcastically, "didn't want to give Guy the best slot because he's under a fog of suspicion."

Lark rolled her eyes and flipped her hair back. "Who knows anything about this Knapp guy?"

Rachel saw Dorothy wince. Was it Lark's use of the word *guy,* or because Knapp's name triggered a reaction?

"He's the digiscoping teacher." Rachel set her binoculars on the dresser. "I'm taking his class on Thursday, and they're showing his film, *A Bird's-Eye View,* that night. It costs ten dollars, and everyone's invited. I've heard it's a great film." It had been showing at the Esquire Theater, but Rachel hadn't had the chance to go. "According to the write-up in the festival brochure, all proceeds are being donated to the conservation of painted bunting breeding territory."

She may as well have been talking to the wall, for all the reaction she got.

Dorothy crossed to the window. "I'll bet Guy is disappointed at not getting back the Saturday slot."

That drew a reaction from Cecilia. "Maybe they thought he wouldn't be around on Saturday."

"That's downright mean," said Dorothy.

"Oh my, it was meant to be a joke."

"A bad one," Dorothy shot back.

"That's right, I forgot he was your boyfriend."

Was Cecilia jealous? Rachel wondered. She had been the one pushing Dorothy to engage.

"He's not my boyfriend. He's my friend."

"Whom half the people here think is guilty of killing Becker," added Cecilia. "Who knows, with that kind of a rap I might cut out early."

Judging from the gaggle of admirers surrounding him in the hotel lobby, being a suspected murderer hadn't lessened Saxby's cachet. But he did look up, directly at Dorothy, as the women descended the stairs to head for the banquet. Dorothy's face glowed.

Cecilia made a small noise in her throat, and then said she had to get some water.

Rachel moved closer to Lark.

"I think Cecilia may be a little jealous," said Lark, giving voice to Rachel's earlier assessment. She sounded critical, which Rachel thought funny, seeing as how Lark had never wanted Dorothy and Guy to hook up in the first place.

Below them, Rachel could see Saxby pushing his way through the crowd. He seemed unhurried, but clearly on a beeline for Dorothy. He stopped to exchange a few words with one person or to pat another on the shoulder, but when he reached Dorothy he placed both hands on her shoulders and ignored the rest of the room.

"What is he up to now?" asked Lark.

"Don't be so suspicious," said Rachel. "I think he really likes her."

"Or else . . ." Lark dropped her voice. "Did it ever occur to you that maybe he did kill Becker, and that he thinks Dorothy knows something."

"I was there, too. He's not trying to cozy up to me," said Rachel.

"Still, I'm not convinced we should let them out of our sight."

"Cecilia seems to agree with you," said Rachel, pointing to Cecilia approaching stage left. When she reached Dorothy, she linked her elbow with her sister's and hung on, thwarting Dorothy's valiant attempts to extract her arm.

"For what it's worth," said Rachel, "I don't think he killed Becker."

"Why not?"

"Even if he wanted to, I don't think he has the guts."

Saxby joined them on the ride to the convention center, and tagged along toward the ballroom. It was adjacent to the Nest, which was open for business. Rachel noted that extra guards had been posted at the doors. The murder scene had been cleaned up, the removable walls were gone, and the vendors plied their wares with zeal. They'd missed out on half a day's sales. No one seemed too overly concerned with Becker's death, though it was the topic on everyone lips.

"So what are you planning?" asked Lark. "Are we taking Dorothy's case?"

Rachel thought about feigning ignorance, and then capitulated. "For Dorothy's sake, I think we have to help clear him. She is over the moon for him . . ." She raised her hand to keep Lark from speaking. "And it's my fault. It's also our fault he's the prime suspect."

"Like you have that much control. Dorothy seemed destined to fall for him anyway, and he would have been the prime suspect no matter what. He's the only one with a motive. Stop beating yourself up."

Rachel looked at her friend. "You're right, but I'd still like to know who killed Becker."

Lark shook her head. "Rae, it's one thing to solve a murder when you're in familiar territory and all you have to do to clear somebody is, say, scale a mountain or two. But here —"

Rachel interrupted by grabbing Lark's arm. "Is that who I think it is?"

A woman in a black tank tap and black shorts stood next to a Lucy Bell foot massage chair.

"If you think it's the grieving widow."

Rachel watched the woman take a chair. "You know what? They've got two chairs set up, and there isn't a line. I think I'm in the mood for a Lucy Bell foot massage."

Lark groaned.

CHAPTER 8

Lark disappeared to find Cecilia and Dorothy, while Rachel made for the empty pedicure chair. She forked over ten dollars before peeling off her shoes and socks and climbing up in the chair next to Sonja.

"Talk about feeling self-conscious," said Rachel. Now she knew how Reggie and Beau's birds must feel. A few women cast longing glances, but most of the birders heading into the ballroom gawked and whispered to each other as they passed by, no doubt wondering why the grieving widow was getting a pedicure. Sonja Becker seemed to be handling this by keeping her eyes shut while her feet soaked.

Rachel had to admit that the warm, oiled water felt very relaxing.

"Mrs. Becker," Rachel said, almost hesitantly. "Sonja, isn't it?"

The dark-haired woman didn't open her eyes. "Do I know you?"

"We met at dinner the other night," Rachel said. "I'm here on a freelance basis, working up an article for *Birds of a Feather* magazine, and I wanted to convey my condolences."

"Thank you," Sonja Becker replied without much interest.

Rachel gritted her teeth. Now what? She'd made a fool of herself, not to mention exaggerated her connection with *Birds of a Feather* magazine and all she had gotten for it was a faint "Thank you."

Well, what had she expected? That the grieving widow would pour out her soul while a redheaded Lucy Bell conventioneer in a pink smock rubbed cinnamon-scented foot oil into her soles?

"This is nice, isn't it?" said Rachel. "Although I think they could have put up a curtain or something. It's kind of weird to get a pedicure in public like this." *Especially weird when your husband has just been murdered.*

Shouldn't she be making funeral arrangements or something?

"It's all the same to me," said Sonja, without opening her eyes. "They can stare if they want."

Rachel decided she was using the kindergarten approach. Nobody could see her if she kept her eyes shut.

"Excuse me." A different Lucy Bell lady handed Rachel a color wheel of nail polish, and tried pushing another into Sonja's hands. "While you're soaking, you can pick your colors."

"Black," Sonja said, pushing the color wheel back. "I've just lost my husband. Black for the widow."

The Lucy Bell lady opened her mouth, and then turned to Rachel with a helpless look that seemed to ask if Sonja was for real. Rachel nodded confirmation.

"That's awful!" said the redhead. "I'm so sorry."

"Don't be," said Sonja. "Paul was an idiot."

"He was a highly respected birder," said Rachel, trying to say something positive. "Plus a leader in the environmental movement."

"An idiot," repeated Sonja. "I wouldn't be at all surprised if he wasn't killed by an irate husband — except the sort of thing he was attracted to wasn't even old enough to be married."

Rachel swallowed. "Are you saying he took an interest in his students?" She wondered if Sonja realized that gave her a motive for murder.

"Them, too," Sonja said.

"Ma'am," said the redhead. "I know this is a difficult time, but begging your pardon, could I recommend something a little more subtle than black? There is this nice neutral shade called Bare Maximum."

"Whatever," Sonja said. "Although it's not much of a mourning color, is it?"

The Lucy Bell shot a horrified glance at Rachel.

"I'll try it," said Rachel, handing back her color wheel. "I normally go with red, but then I've never had a Lucy Bell pedicure before."

"I don't see what's wrong with black," said Sonja. She lifted a sports bottle and took a deep draft, then leaned her head back again. "Did you ever wonder why doctors always tell you to drink water? Whatever climate you go to, it's the same. If you go to Arizona they say, drink lots of water, it's a dry climate, and you'll lose body fluids. If you go to the coast they say, drink lots of water, it's a humid climate, and you'll lose body fluids. Where can you go where you don't lose body fluids?"

"You've got me there." Rachel glanced at the sports bottle. She had a sneaking suspicion the liquid inside it wasn't water. Well, people dealt with serious loss in different ways.

"What were we talking about?" asked Sonja. "Oh, yes, how Paul was an idiot. Let me count the ways."

Rachel's pink-smocked Lucy Bell lady began sawing away at Rachel's heels with a file. The sensation was not unpleasant — in fact, it tickled. She pressed the back of her hand to her mouth and concentrated on what Sonja was saying.

"He couldn't get ahead. He always let people take advantage of him. You could always count on Paul to be on the side that got shafted."

"I was under the impression he'd done pretty well," said Rachel. "He seemed to be well-respected." Or had she already said that? She thought she had.

"Oh, sure. He and his trust fund did fine. Inherited money is always a mistake. It makes you soft, afraid to stand up for yourself."

This didn't sound like the Paul Becker that Rachel had seen insisting on being the Saturday keynote speaker. It didn't sound like the people she knew who'd inherited money, either.

"He always opened his big mouth too early, jumped on the wrong bandwagon," continued Sonja. "Of course, he would eventually realize it, then backpedal. Like flipping on that land trade."

"I thought he was against it." If he was for it, that might change the suspect list.

"He *was* against it," said Sonja. "But then, after he went out with Chuck, he was all for it."

"Chuck Knapp?"

"The filmmaker."

Now Rachel knew who Becker had gone birding with, but she still didn't know what their great discovery in the swamp was. She wondered if he'd told Sonja. "Did they find something out there?"

"I've got no idea," said Sonja. "Did I mention that Paul was an idiot? Given enough time, he probably would have flipped back. That was his nature, wishy-washy. But he ran out of time."

Rachel thought about that as the Lucy Bell lady at her feet delivered an excellent massage. Wishy-washy, Sonja had said. He would have flipped back, but he ran out of time. Maybe that was the point?

"Speaking of backpedaling," said Sonja. "This is not to say that Paul wasn't excellent at the one thing he did well. Do you know, he had spotted more birds than anyone in the history of the world. At that, he was supreme." She took another swig from her sports bottle. "He was better than anyone. He was a hell of a lot better than that boss of his, that's for sure. It's just a very odd thing to be really good at, don't you think?"

"I don't know. I've been working hard to get better at it myself," said Rachel. She watched as the Lucy Bell ladies rubbed cinnamon-scented foot cream into her feet and Sonja's.

"Of course you'd be one of them." Sonja sounded tired. "I just don't understand it. If you've seen one bird, you've seen them all. Oh, and Paul wasn't half bad at golf, either. Another thing I don't get. I guess if there's a place in heaven for idiots there will be a golf course with lots of birds on it."

"I don't get golf either," admitted Rachel. *And I don't get you.* Roger was an idiot, and Roger loved golf, too. But, if someone had killed Roger before she'd had a chance to divorce him, she'd still have been sorry. Wouldn't she?

"Don't twitch," Sonja's Lucy Bell lady ordered. "You're twitching."

"Well *excuuuuse* me," replied Sonja.

Rachel tried to relax. "I've heard Paul was working on a book. Do you think it will still be published?"

"I'm thinking it ought to be published very soon," Sonja said. "But here's a case in point. Here is a perfect opportunity for some great publicity. But did he get the damn thing finished in time for it to be in print. Can you imagine what a signed copy would bring now?"

Rachel drew in her breath. Any sympathy she might have felt for Becker's widow evaporated.

"Of course, he would have finished it, it his department head hadn't stolen his original research," added Sonja. "The creep even stole the title. Luckily, you can't copyright titles, so we're using it anyway. *A Sacrifice of Buntings*. Doesn't that sound more like a baseball book? Another sport I don't get."

Rachel wanted to pop right out of her chair and e-mail Kirk. "Are you talking about Guy Saxby?"

It had to be. That was the title of Saxby's book.

"The one and only," said Sonja. "He even stole the title. Luckily you can't copyright titles." She repeated, word for word, what she'd just said, except this time she called it *A Sacrifice of Puntings*.

"There you go!" chirped the redhead.

"Now don't put on your shoes for half an hour!"

Rachel's Lucy Bell lady patted her calf. *Great,* so now she was supposed to wander around the Nest barefoot, holding her hiking boots?

"If you want something to do while you wait, we have a small display set up," suggested the Lucy Bell lady. "Or you could get a facial! That will give you plenty of time for your polish to dry. Here's a coupon!"

Sonja had finally opened her eyes and was staring at her feet. "Good grief, she did it. She really did it. She painted my toenails black!"

Rachel passed on the facial and vacated the chair for the next client. She weighed the risks of ruining her pedicure versus sharing her news, and decided she could always repaint her toenails at a more propitious moment. Nobody was going to see her toes anyway.

Under the glare of the Lucy Bell lady, she slipped on her socks and stuffed her feet into her boots, while Sonja sacheted barefoot toward the ballroom. Rachel headed to the Nest, and found Lark, Cecilia, and Dorothy admiring a Leica scope across from Beau and Reggie's Birds of Prey exhibit.

Rachel looked for blood on the floor, or any sign of what had happened there just a few hours ago, but the booth was white-washed.

"The show is starting in eight minutes," Cecilia said. "We thought we'd catch it this time. We may not get another chance."

"Guy asked me to wait for him here. He had some business to attend to with Evan Kearns."

I'll bet he did, thought Rachel.

She signaled a huddle. "Paul Becker had changed his position on the land trade."

"So?" said Dorothy. "Lots of people change their minds about things. Besides, what's it matter? He's already dead."

"Except that it changes our suspect list," said Rachel.

Lark frowned. "How so?"

"Because he was against the trade before, which is the premise we used when we started to list everyone. Now we need to look at people who might be against the trade and or be angry because he switched sides."

"What would have changed his mind?" asked Dorothy. "He seemed dead set against it the other night. He said he'd always been against it." Dorothy attempted to mimic Becker. " 'While one area would be protected, the other area would lose its protection.' "

"It must have to do with the mysterious treasure," said Cecilia.

"Or maybe he found out who was making the other offer to the Andersons, and it changed his mind," said Dorothy. "Maybe what the developer plans to do to the swamp is worse than losing eighty acres of nesting habitat for the painted bunting on Hyde Island."

"Do you want some good news?" Rachel asked. "I think I know how to find out what Becker saw in that swamp. Sonja told me the name of the person he went birding with that day. He was with Chuck Knapp."

"The filmmaker?" Lark looked surprised. "That might explain why Knapp is now assigned to the Saturday-night keynote spot."

"And there's one more thing." Rachel glanced at Dorothy. "If Saxby is the Indiana Jones of the birding world, according to his wife, Paul Becker was the James Bond."

CHAPTER 9

They needed to talk to Chuck Knapp.

Rachel thought about it all through dinner on Tuesday night, and considered bagging out on Wednesday's Little St. Simons trip. She figured with most of the birders out in the field, it might be easier to corner him during the day. Provided he wasn't out on a trip.

Lark and Cecilia wouldn't hear of it.

"You can't miss Little St. Simons, Rae," said Lark. "I guarantee we'll see more birds out there than anywhere else we go this trip."

"Besides," said Cecilia, "the police are doing their job investigating this horrible crime. If Guy is innocent, they will clear him."

Rachel noticed her choice of words, but then Dorothy concurred, so Rachel set the alarm for 4:30 a.m.

Little St. Simons was ten thousand acres

of pristine barrier island accessible only by boat. It was exactly the same amount of land the Andersons had put up for trade, except Rachel couldn't believe the swampland would measure up by comparison. Little St. Simons was one of those rare places on earth — secluded, unspoiled, and beautiful.

The boat departed Hampton River Club Marina and churned its way through pristine marsh land to Barge Landing. There the birdwatchers were loaded into the backs of two pickup trucks and ferried along a sandy road through live oaks draped in Spanish moss. Rachel sat on the tailgate, sandwiched between Lark and Dorothy, and imagined the land to be much like this when it was occupied by the Guale Indians. The only traces she could see of modern civilization were the small grouping of buildings that comprised Little St. Simons Lodge.

According to the guidebooks, in the 1770s, a U.S. senator from South Carolina purchased six hundred acres of the island for a rice plantation. Eventually, he bought up the island, but when the end of the Civil War sent the plantation culture of Georgia's sea islands into a tail spin, his family sold out to the Eagle Pencil Company, sight unseen. The pencil company's plan was to harvest cedar trees for pencil production; but the trees proved too damaged by wind and salt to make quality pencils, so the owner of the company, Philip Berolzheimer, traveled to Little St. Simons to salvage his loss. Instead, hypnotized by the island's beauty, he built a private hunting lodge, allowing only his family and closest friends from New York to visit.

In 1979, Berolzheimer's descendants opened the island to the public, but even then it was protected. The family served as stewards of the land, hiring educated staff to conduct tours, and thus limiting the impact of tourism. Little St. Simons truly was an island paradise.

Rachel gaped at the scenery as they passed through a gnarled canopy of oaks, cedars, pines, and wild magnolias. Pine warblers flitted overhead — a stocky bird, olive with a yellow chest, it had two distinct wingbands. Tracking a flash of bright yellow, she spotted a prothonotary warbler, its golden head and chest easily discernable among the branches.

"Listen," said the trip leader.

A clear whistle descended from the treetops, rising on the last note: *teeew, teew, teeew, teew, tuwee.*

"That is a yellow-throated warbler."

"That would be a life bird for me," said Dorothy.

"I have it already," announced Cecilia.

"Then we'll be tied up at six hundred and ten birds each."

"If you find it," said Cecilia.

It took Dorothy a minute and a half to locate the bird. Perched high in a tree, it belted out its song. "Right there."

Rachel studied the bird, and then a flash of blue moved through her peripheral vision. She searched the trees to the left, and found a very small bird hidden in the branches. Blue gray with white wing bars, it had limited yellow on its throat, pale eye crescents, and black- and rust-colored bands on its chest. "What bird is that?" She pointed to the upper branches. "About eleven o'clock in that oak tree. It's fairly well-hidden in the branches and leaves."

Zz-zz-zzz-zzzeee-wup.

"Good catch," said the leader. "That's a Northern parula. They're common in the summer here, but they like to stay hidden. Can someone get a scope on that bird for us?"

Four people obliged, including Rachel, with Lark's help.

"That makes six hundred and eleven for me," Dorothy crowed.

145

Rachel wondered when this had become about listing. Before this trip, the sisters had always just been excited to see the birds. Now it seemed like a major competition.

"It's beautiful," said Rachel. She tried snapping a picture, holding her digital camera to the scope's eyepiece. Tomorrow she'd get a real lesson. "Anyone else care to look?"

Several people stepped forward, and then Lark took a turn. Both Dorothy and Cecilia were too wrapped up writing in their field notebooks to take more than a quick peek.

"On this trip, I'm going to pull ahead," said Dorothy.

"Oh my, Dot, I suppose we'll just have to see about that."

The trucks moved on, snaking along a small creek and stopping beside a small pond.

"What's the name of this lake?" asked Lark.

The guide looked at her funny. "Where are you from?"

"Colorado."

"That explains it," he said. "Around here, we call this a pond. East Myrtle Pond. There a bird tower you can climb over there. We'll be looking for wading birds here. Egrets. Ibis. If you're lucky, a roseate spoonbill."

"I don't have that," said Cecilia.

"Me, either," Dorothy replied.

They did get lucky. On the far side of the pond, three large pink birds swung their spatulate bills from side to side in the water.

From the tower, they quickly added to their list: white ibis, glossy ibis, wood storks, great and snowy egrets. To the north, second-growth cyprus served as a rookery. The trees were full of nesting birds — wood storks, yellow-crowned and black-crowned night herons, egrets, black vultures, and anhingas. Overhead an osprey streaked toward its nest, while a bald eagle made lazy circles toward space.

"Keep your eyes open," instructed the guide. "You may see lots of other critters in here, like raccoons, opossums, and bobcats. It's also prime habitat for alligators and snakes."

"What kind of snakes?" asked Rachel, unable to squelch her squeamishness.

"Mostly cottonmouths and rattlesnakes."

After that, Rachel spent a lot more time watching where she stepped. She noticed Lark treading carefully, too.

After an hour, they loaded up the trucks, skirted the salt marshes, adding a reddish egret and small blue heron to their list, and then stormed the beach.

The shorebirds were plentiful as well — Wilson's plovers, piping plovers, American oystercatchers, black-necked stilts, American avocets, whimbrels, long-billed curlews, and red-knots galore.

Little St. Simons had proved to be a birder's paradise. As a group, the total field trip count was ninety-two species, of which Rachel counted sixty. Dorothy had seen all ninety-two, and Cecilia managed ninety. By the end, Dorothy stood one bird ahead on the life list.

Rachel felt sad to leave. There was something spellbinding and slightly primitive about the Little St. Simons and its miles of coastline. It made Hyde Island, even with its murder, seem positively civilized.

Saxby was waiting for them back at the hotel, and while the others agreed to join him for dinner, Rachel begged off. She was tired, but, more important, she had an early-morning workshop the next day: digiscoping with Chuck Knapp.

One of the things she remembered from her college news reporting class was it's best to arm yourself with knowledge before an interview. If she planned on talking with Knapp the next day, she wanted to be prepared.

First off, if Becker and Knapp had seen an interesting bird — one that would change their mind about the land swap — what could it have been?

It couldn't be any of the birds she had seen. Even the rare ones from the field trips were common enough to the area not to make news. Rachel surfed the Web, pored over her guidebooks, and found that several endangered birds made the swamp their habitat. Hadn't Saxby said he'd spotted a nesting red-cockaded woodpecker in the area? Or what about something like the ivory-billed woodpecker? The bird was thought to be extinct until 2005, when it was spotted in an Arkansas swamp. Maybe Becker and Knapp had found one here. It was the same sort of habitat, and the bird used to live in this region.

Of course, their "treasure" didn't have to be a bird. Other animals, plenty of them, made the swamp their home: spiders, snakes, various kinds of biting flies. After reading about them, Rachel made a mental note to be sure to take the insect repellant on Friday. No way did she want to became a meal for the yellow flies.

Becker's book might have provided some insight. Too bad it hadn't been published in time.

Too bad he was dead.

Exhausting her search on the creatures at the swamp, Rachel turned to researching Knapp. She read his bio in the program, read his bio on his Website, but otherwise couldn't dig up much more than the fact that he was both a wildlife filmmaker and photographer. Something she already knew.

Rachel checked her e-mail and found a message waiting from Kirk.

find out anything more on saxby? the birds are thriving here, but the species have changed some. sort of like what happens when there's a wildfire. wish I was there. kirk

Rachel pictured him in his khaki shorts, and then typed:

I'm not so sure. Paul Becker, one of the keynote speakers, was murdered. Dorothy and I were questioned. Saxby is the prime suspect. He obviously has something big to reveal, but he refuses to dish. Becker had something big up his sleeve, too. I'm beginning to wonder if it's one and the same. There's a filmmaker named Chuck Knapp who might know something. I'm going digiscoping with him tomorrow. I'll be in touch.

She paused, and then added:

Thinking of you. Rachel

and hit Send.

The others came back from dinner with Saxby's tales of the interrogation. The detective had grilled him relentlessly, convinced he had been there. Saxby had stuck to his guns, and insisted he never made it inside the Nest. Finally, they had released him.

"I told you, he didn't do it," crowed Dorothy.

"He's still their prime suspect," Cecilia pointed out.

"Thank you for your input," snapped Dorothy.

"Why?" asked Rachel. "If the guard turned him away, and they can't prove he was there . . ."

"The guard doesn't remember talking to him," explained Dorothy. "And we said he was there, or he was supposed to be there."

"The detective admitted to Guy . . ." Rachel noticed Lark used his first name. ". . . That the shots came from outside," she continued. "He thinks the person arguing with Becker might have slipped out the doors and shot him back through the glass."

"That's absurd," said Dorothy. "We would have heard the door open."

"Maybe, or maybe not," said Rachel. "That would have been about the time I bumped into that rack, and the scuffle came before the shot."

"He didn't do it." Dorothy's voice verged on tears.

Rachel patted the end of her bed. "Sit down. I've been doing some research."

She told them what little she had discovered, and then asked them what they thought of her endangered species theory.

"It makes sense," said Dorothy quickly.

Too quickly? Rachel wondered.

"Oh my," said Cecilia. "I think you girls are grasping at straws."

"Seriously, Cec," said Dorothy. "A find like the ivory-billed woodpecker would give someone lot of notoriety. Look at the man who found the one in Arkansas. If Knapp and Becker had one clearly on film —"

"It would upstage Guy," said Lark, "giving him an even stronger reason to have it out for Becker."

Dorothy stiffened. "Are you insinuating that Guy Saxby would kill Becker to steal his film?"

"I don't think that's what she was saying," said Rachel. "If that were the case, he'd have to kill Knapp, too. But" — How to divulge this? — "Sonja Becker did say that years ago Saxby had stolen her husband's work, and then published it as his own."

Dorothy stiffened. "That is a lie!"

"There is no way to prove it, one way or the other," said Rachel. "Especially with Becker dead."

The four of them fell silent. Lark perched on her bed, sitting opposite Dorothy. Cecilia sat in a chair by the window. Dorothy stared at her hands in her lap, and Rachel could feel her heart breaking.

"Look, Dorothy, I'm with you," said Rachel. "I don't think Guy killed Becker either." Now she was calling him Guy. What she didn't say was that she didn't believe Saxby had the backbone to kill anyone. "Let's make a suspect list, and this time let's write down the names and their motives."

Rummaging around on the bedside table, Rachel produced a pad of paper and a pen, and poked Dorothy with the end of the pen.

Dorothy drew a deep breath. "There's Wolcott," she said.

"Except I think he wants the trade," said Lark. "Remember how he acted at dinner the other evening? He played it cautiously, but he seemed firmly in the Andersons' camp."

"Agreed," said Rachel. "He might not have known Becker switched sides. We didn't know until Sonja let it slip." Rachel wrote down Wolcott's name.

"He'd need a strong reason to want the trade," said Lark. "Strong enough to kill over."

Rachel couldn't think of anything.

Dorothy's head came up. "What if he has some development plans no one knows about?"

"That's good," said Cecilia.

"What are we talking about?" asked Lark. "More hotel beds. I'll bet the Andersons would be against that."

"Unless they were working with him," said Cecilia.

"Like in *Murder on the Orient Express*." Rachel recalled Agatha Christie's famous novel made into a movie in 1974 starring Albert Finney and Lauren Bacall. Maybe it was a conspiracy. She scribbled a note beside Wolcott's name: CHECK OUT ULTERIOR MOTIVES.

Lark kiboshed their excitement. "I don't see Wolcott as the murdering type."

"There's a type?" asked Dorothy. "If so,

Guy certainly doesn't fit, yet everyone seems willing enough to suspect him."

Rachel jumped in to head off an argument. "Let's stay focused on the list, okay? Who else had a motive to kill Becker?"

"The Andersons," said Lark.

"Again, like Wolcott, only if they didn't know he had switched camps." Rachel scribbled another note. CHECK OUT OFFER ON SWAMPLAND. Maybe there was something there that would give them a clue.

"Then again," said Lark. "Either way they come out ahead. Maybe they don't belong on the list."

"How about the Carters?" suggested Cecilia. "Those boys seemed quite protective of their swamp treasures."

Rachel scribbled the names on her pad, and then nibbled the end of her pen.

"Fancy didn't seem too worried," said Lark.

"Of course not," said Dorothy. "Like the Andersons, either way she sells her land for a profit."

"It's not always about money, Dot."

Rachel wrote, CHECK ON MARKET PRICE AT CARTERS' ACREAGE. That should be easy enough. A local real estate site on the Internet should give them a close approximation.

Lark twisted her braid, and turned to Rachel. "What about someone other than Guy who might have a reason to want him dead?"

"I have Sonja on the list."

"But what about someone else?"

"How about Beau and Reggie?" Dorothy stood and paced the length of the floor. "Maybe Becker figured out they were obtaining their birds illegally."

Lark looked as skeptical as Rachel felt. "I'll add them, but I think that's a stretch." Her notes were getting extensive.

"I don't buy that either," said Lark. "I know what Aunt Miriam has to go through to maintain the licensing for the Raptor House. Those two would be under a lot of scrutiny, especially if they have questionable backgrounds."

CHECK OUT BEAU'S AND REGGIE'S BIRDS OF PREY FOUNDATION.

"Maybe we should add the protestors." They seemed peaceful, but they were passionate in their beliefs, passionate enough to stand outside twenty-four/seven and picket in front of the Hyde Island Club Hotel.

"What about Chuck Knapp?" asked Lark. *What about him?* He and Becker both had an interest in the film. Had he and Becker been arguing about the tape?

"And don't forget the developer who wants to acquire the swampland," said Cecilia.

And ex-lovers or current lovers. There was any number of people who might want Becker dead.

Rachel reached for her computer. "Let's start with who we have. Let's see what we can find out about Wolcott."

"Have we researched Becker?" asked Cecilia.

"And how about Guy?" Lark added, with a glance at Dorothy.

Rachel had done extensive research on Saxby. Kirk had done even more. She had read nearly every magazine article ever written about the man. Of those, none had suggested he'd stolen his grad student's research, but then, most were meant to be favorable. She wondered what Kirk would think when she told him the truth about his icon.

"Why not," said Dorothy. She shot Lark a glare, the kind that had made generations of high-school students go quiet and attentive. "Look him up."

"Who? Saxby?" said Rachel.

"Sure, maybe we can find a shot of him

without a shirt on!"

Cecilia's mouth dropped open. Lark and Rachel laughed — Rachel a little nervously. She was afraid Dorothy was serious.

She started typing "Victor Wolcott" into the search engine, but Dorothy insisted.

"Try Guy first."

Cecilia and Lark nodded. Were they calling her bluff?

Rachel started over, aware that the others had gathered around her. Three heads leaned toward the screen of her laptop.

"Oh my," Cecelia said. "He's taught at Stanford, and —"

"Died five years ago," Dorothy said dryly.

"There must be another one," said Cecilia.

"You think?" Lark drawled.

Rachel scrolled through the entries.

"That's him!" Dorothy pointed to the screen.

Rachel clicked on the link, and they waited as his photograph loaded. He still had his shirt on, but it was a nice shirt with a tie, and he was smiling at a woman who looked very familiar.

"The *Today Show*." Dorothy sighed. "I don't think I've ever met anyone who's been on the *Today Show* before."

Rachel clicked on another Web page and

scrolled down.

"Sure you have," said Cecilia. "Remember, we met that basketball player, Magic something, and we saw Liz Taylor eating in the restaurant at the Drummond. And what about that bicycle rider. He was eating at the Drummond, too. Not with Liz, but —"

"Okay, I surrender. Let's just say, I've never had drinks with anyone who was on the *Today Show* before. That was a first for me."

"Stop there," Lark commanded. "Isn't that Guy with Paul Becker?"

Rachel expanded the image. Becker sat on a stage, just behind Guy, who stood in front of a microphone addressing a crowd. Guy's mouth was open and one hand was extended before him. Becker studied him with a scowl.

"Can you read the banner behind them?" Lark asked.

"Not any better than you can." Frankly, Rachel was having trouble seeing around Cecilia's head. "I only see two letters, and they probably aren't the most important ones." Rachel clicked on the text.

"Oh my, that's too small to read," said Cecilia.

"It's a review of Guy's book," said Dorothy. "It looks like a wonderful review, too."

"But what's going on in that picture?" asked Lark. "Becker doesn't look happy."

Rachel ran her hands through her hair. "This isn't getting us anywhere. Let me try Wolcott."

"Try Becker," said Dorothy.

Rachel complied.

"Oh, he's got a nice bod," said Cecilia when a picture of a body builder flashed on the screen. "Maybe you'll get a picture of him with his shirt off."

"It's a common name," said Rachel, suppressing a laugh. No way did she want to egg Cecilia on.

There were a lot of Beckers. They ran track in high schools, addressed Lions Clubs in obscure cities, and had Web pages featuring their teenaged angst.

"Try adding the word *bird*," suggested Lark.

This popped up with a Web page with the same photo of Saxby and Becker, but this Web page guided her to a discussion forum. She clicked on that before the photo had loaded, and at the top of the page was a thread discussing Becker's death. *Now, that's more like it.*

"He seems pretty well-regarded," said Lark, as Rachel scrolled through several messages expressing sorrow and surprise.

"That's interesting." Cecilia leaned her head in closer, blocking Rachel's view altogether. "Someone is saying Paul Becker's book would have been published years earlier except his department head at the time stole all his research, forcing Becker to start over from scratch."

Rachel shifted uncomfortably. "That's exactly what Sonja told me. She said he'd even stolen Becker's title." What Rachel didn't rub in was that, according to Sonja, the department head in question was Guy.

"Oh my, that's bad." Cecilia pointed to the next post. "It says here —"

Dorothy cut her sister off. "It's an opinion on a message board, that's all. It doesn't make it fact."

"Wait! This is getting interesting, Dot. Rachel, scroll down."

"Let's come back to it later."

Before Cecilia could protest, Rachel hit the Back button and bookmarked the page. It was clear Dorothy wasn't ready to hear the message. Then again, at some point she would have to face the music that Guy Saxby wasn't all that he was cracked up to be.

CHAPTER 10

The others called it a night, but Rachel stayed up and checked out a few more Websites before going to bed. She learned a couple of interesting things.

The real estate Fancy and her boys were sitting on was worth somewhere in the range of thirty-five hundred to over six thousand dollars an acre, maybe more if the stakes for access to Swamper's Island were high enough. That meant, provided the Carters got top dollar, they would walk away with between one hundred seventy-five thousand to over three hundred thousand dollars. Not bad for fifty or so acres of undeveloped swampland, and enough money to serve as motive.

The search on Wolcott turned up his resume, address, telephone number, what hotels and ice cream shops he lived close to, and not much else.

As expected, Beau and Reggie checked

out clean.

Aware it was late Rachel finally logged off and turned out the light. She dreamed of Geechee houses, Trula, and *hudu* warnings, and awoke in the morning still tired, with the nagging feeling that Paul Becker had been trying to tell her something.

With very little sleep the night before, the morning session of the digiscoping workshop came early. The murder was a buzz on everyone's lips, and Rachel arrived with time to spare, coffee in hand, prepared to eavesdrop. She ended up at a table next to the protest leader.

He was cuter up close, she decided, and his hazel eyes twinkled when he realized she recognized him.

"A birder by day," she said.

"Protestor by night." He reached out a strong, lean hand. "Liam Kelly."

They shook, then Chuck Knapp arrived and all conversation ceased.

She found the information he gave them on cameras and scopes interesting, but with her background in graphic production the stuff on how to frame a shot, composition and color, she already knew quite a bit.

"Do you find this boring?"

Was it that obvious?

Realizing that the person who had spoken wasn't her tablemate, Rachel was startled out of her stupor to find everyone filing out for a break and Chuck Knapp standing in front of her table.

"No," she stammered, facing his glower. "I just . . ." How not to sound like an idiot? "I work in graphics, so I know a lot about what you were teaching. I'm looking forward to getting out in the field this afternoon."

"Good. I was worried." He smiled then, and it softened his looks. Dark curly hair bumped the collar of his beige shirt, and his blue eyes were sharp and appraising. "One question: If you know all of this, why take my class?"

"You're a legend." She smiled, hoping he would bask in her flattery. Instead, he acted annoyed.

"And here I thought maybe you were interested in photographing birds."

"I am," she said, realizing her mistake. "Very interested. I just spent two days in the field, first on Sapelo Island, and yesterday on Little St. Simons. On Friday, I'm canoeing in the Okefenokee Swamp. I'd like to be able to take some pictures using my scope."

She noticed his eyes widened when she mentioned the swamp. Maybe now was the time to ask him about his adventure with Becker.

"I hear you had a great day birding the Okefenokee last week."

Knapp's face shuttered.

"I'm sorry about your friend."

"He was a good birder. We had some luck."

"What did you see?" She tried sounding nonchalant, and didn't succeed.

"Why do I get the impression you're prying?"

Rachel had the good sense to look down. "Let me be straight, Mr. Knapp. I am here to learn how to digiscope, but you're right, I am prying." She explained about Dorothy's infatuation with Saxby, and her own worry that she was partly responsible for getting her friend mixed up in something sinister.

"You should worry. Guy Saxby's a thief."

"Why do you say that?" When he didn't answer, she filled in the blanks. "Because he stole Becker's thesis and published it as his own?"

His blue eyes met hers squarely. "If you know, why do you trust him?"

"I didn't say I trusted him. I'm just not convinced he's a murderer. Are you?"

"I don't know what I think about that. I

do know I have something he wants."

On that note, Knapp clammed up and refused to say anything more. After lunch, he led them out to the golf course.

Standing at the edge of the ninth hole, he pointed toward the shrub habitat, which stretched toward the ocean in the distance. "This is the prime nesting habitat of the painted bunting on Hyde Island."

Behind them a golfer yelled, "Fore!" and Rachel instinctively ducked. She noticed several others did the same. Knapp remained upright.

"Isn't this the land the Andersons are hoping to trade for?" Rachel asked, raising her head in anticipation of his answer.

"Yes." He drew the group closer in, either to make it easier to talk or to protect them from the golfers, then asked, "How many of you know how much land is needed to support one hundred breeding pairs of painted buntings?"

No one offered a guess.

"Twelve hundred." He paused to let the number sink in.

"Any twelve hundred?" asked a man wearing a T-shirt emblazoned with Lydia Thompson's painted bunting. A local artist, she had a knack for realism.

"No," answered Knapp. He waved his

arms at the tangle of trees at the edge of the green, like a magician revealing a hidden treasure. "The painted bunting can utilize a variety of habitats. But territorial males occur in highest density in open, grassy areas with abundant shrubs and a few scattered trees." His hands painted the landscape in front of them. "Painted buntings like open pine-oak forests with some canopy remaining." He pointed to the treetops. "Forests with abundant grasses and shrubs." He pointed to the ground. "That's what the birds eat, wild grasses and weed seeds. That's why this habitat is so important for shrub-scrub nesting birds such as the white-eyed vireo, northern cardinal, and painted bunting.

"Another thing, pay attention to the water. Painted buntings breed where there are wetlands or salt marshes nearby. Here a small creek runs to the sea, and there are salt marshes right over there." He pointed. "This land is so exceptional, it supports double its share of nesting painted buntings."

He had made a great case against the trade.

The man whose shirt Rachel had admired earlier nodded in agreement. Rachel made a mental note to purchase a shirt just like his before leaving for home.

A young girl in a tennis visor asked, "What does a painted bunting nest look like?"

Knapp seemed pleased with the question. "They're a deep cup nest made of woven grass, usually found in a bush or vine tangle about three to six feet off the ground. Rarely, you might find a nest buried in Spanish moss at heights up to twenty-three to twenty-six feet, but the ideal territory is characterized by enough vegetation to support and conceal the nest, several singing perches, and a feeding area for the breeding pair."

"Does their plumage vary?" asked someone else.

"It takes two years for a male to become the brilliantly colored songbird on this man's shirt." Knapp pointed to the gentleman in the Lydia Thompson T-shirt. "The young males and females are green, and much harder to spot."

The questions came faster.

"How many eggs does a painted bunting lay?"

"What is their survival rate?"

"Three to four eggs, and not very good," he answered. "The female incubates the eggs for about eleven to twelve days. Nestlings leave the nest at eight or nine days, and then the male may feed the fledglings if the female begins building a new nest. Last year's study estimated only 20 percent of the breeding pairs produced fledglings."

"Why?" several people asked in unison.

"Predators, weather, and development." His emphasis on the last word seemed driven by anger. If he had found an endangered species on Swamper's Island, it hadn't seemed to sway him from his determination to save the painted buntings' habitat. "That is why we must protect this acreage at all cost, and document its rightful owners making use of the land."

"Fore!"

The word came off like an emphasis, and Rachel didn't have time to duck. A golf ball whizzed past her head. It ricocheted off a tree trunk in front of her, and flushed a colorful bird out of the bushes.

"That's one way to pish," mumbled Knapp.

Then another ball whizzed past. At least she thought it was a ball. With a dull *thunk* it struck the tree, spraying bark in its wake.

That was a bullet.

"Get down," yelled Rachel. It wasn't just golf balls they were dodging. Someone was shooting at them.

Most of the birders dropped to the

ground. Another bullet whizzed overhead. Flat on her stomach, she took shelter behind a bush and tried to peer through the branches and see who was firing. She spotted the muzzle of a rifle in a thick copse of trees on the far side of the green.

By now the golfers had realized someone was firing a gun. They lay prone on the grass, cell phones in hand. Rachel heard sirens in the distance, and the muzzle was gone.

Who was the person shooting at? Chuck Knapp? That seemed the logical conclusion. It made sense that whoever had killed Paul Becker would be after Knapp, too. After all, he had been in the swamp, and he had film to prove it.

The police investigation disrupted the workshop. Each attendee was talked to and dismissed, except for Knapp, Liam Kelly, and Rachel.

"This is ludicrous," said Kelly, waving his sinewy arms. "How can I be standing over here taking fire, and be over there shooting the gun?"

The cop remained deadpan, arms crossed over his chest, his legs spread in a vee. "It could have been one of your protestor friends."

"Then he was shooting too close for my

comfort." Liam shook his head. "Unless you have a reason to detain me further, I'm outta here."

The cop shrugged, pivoted, and opened the way, allowing Liam Kelly to pass.

The skinny black cop was talking to Knapp.

Rachel set up her scope while she waited her turn, and snapped a few pictures. A male painted bunting perched on the highest branch of a nearby bush and belted out his song. She took a myriad of pictures, including some of the painted bunting, common yellowthroats, northern cardinals, cops digging the bullets out of the trees, the copse where the shooter had stood, and some close-ups of Knapp.

"What the hell are you doing?"

Rachel recognized the black cop's voice and let her camera rest. "I figured I might make use of the time, Officer."

"Detective. Detective Stone. Why is it you're always where trouble comes?"

"Just lucky, I guess." She told him what she had seen.

"You're sure it was a rifle?"

"Rifle, shotgun. I don't know exactly what type of gun it was, except that it wasn't a handgun. It had a long barrel."

"And a long range," mused the cop.

"Listen, you be careful."

Did he think the shooter might be after her? Maybe he thought she had seen him that day in the Nest when she and Dorothy had found Becker dead. If so, Dorothy would be in danger as well.

"Are you saying the shooter was shooting at me?"

Detective Stone shrugged. "I'm not saying anything, just suggesting you take care." *Oona mus tek cyear.*

"Did you learn anything?" Dorothy asked the minute Rachel entered the room. The adjacent door to the suites was open, and Cecilia, Dorothy, and Lark were gathered around the table in the sisters' room.

"Only that someone either wants Knapp, me, or one of the birders in our digiscoping class dead." She told them about the shooting.

"Thank God no one was hurt," said Lark.

Dorothy looked pale. "If he was after you . . ."

Rachel patted her hand. Dorothy had put two and two together. "More likely the shooter was after Knapp. He claims he has something Guy Saxby wants. It isn't unconceivable that the shooter wants it, too."

"The film footage?" guessed Cecilia,

excitement humming in her voice.

"He refused to say, but it would be my guess." Rachel dropped the tripod she was lugging on her bed, along with her backpack, and then set her camera on the dresser. "The main thing is we can eliminate some suspects from our list. Chuck Knapp and Liam Kelly, for two." She told the others about sitting next to Liam in class.

"Who else?" asked Dorothy.

"Guy has to stay on the list," said Lark.

Rachel felt sorry for Dorothy, but Lark was right. Saxby wasn't in the clear yet.

"How about the rest of you?" she asked.

"Cecilia and I learned how to properly handle our lists."

"Oh my, are you going to start that again, Dorothy?"

"Admit it, I was right. You can't count a bird until you are able to identify it when you see it."

"It doesn't matter anymore. I've seen the painted bunting and identified it any number of times in the past three days."

"How about you, Lark?" Rachel asked, hoping her answer might spare them more of the sister act. "Did you learn anything?"

"I did." She toyed with the end of her braid, and the sisters stopped bickering.

"Oh my," said Cecilia. "Why didn't you

say something earlier, dear?"

Dorothy scooted her chair forward.

"I took the Waterfowl Identification course, and we were down on the beach. It turns out, according to the workshop leader, the eighty acres included in the land trade extends from the golf course all the way to the sand."

Knapp had indicated the same thing.

"So?" said Dorothy.

"So they're not going to expand the golf course all the way to the beach. It seems there is a plan in the works to develop a boardwalk along the dunes, complete with golf shop, retail stores, restaurants, and bicycle rentals."

"Let me guess," said Rachel. "Wolcott is one of the investors."

"Not technically, but, according to the workshop leader, Wolcott's son-in-law is the developer and his wife will control the concessions."

"In a resort community like this, that could mean a significant sum of money," said Cecilia.

Rachel bobbed her head, as if maybe the motion would help shake the pieces in place. "But how could the Hyde Island Authority allow him to get away with that? Didn't Wolcott say that the Authority has to vote on the land swap? Surely they won't turn a blind eye to any pork tacked onto the deal."

"Unless the Authority thinks it's all part of the golf course concessions," said Lark.

"The important thing," said Dorothy, "is it gives Wolcott a vested interest in seeing that this trade goes through."

The banquet that night was a festive affair, even if the main topic of conversation was Becker's murder and the shooting on the golf course this afternoon. A band had been hired to play Georgia bluegrass while the festivalgoers dined on Cornish game hens and rice pilaf. Rachel noticed Lark and Cecilia both bopped to the beat, but Dorothy spent her time looking around. Most likely searching for Saxby. It wasn't until they were lined up to get into the theater to see Knapp's movie that Saxby appeared.

Placing one hand on Dorothy's shoulder and the other on Rachel's, he said, "You ladies are coming along tomorrow on the Okefenokee field trip, right?"

"We wouldn't miss it," replied Rachel.

Dorothy beamed at the man. "I can hardly wait."

Cecilia and Lark nodded. Rachel noticed

that Cecilia had set her mouth in a hard line.

"Good, very good. But there's been a change at plans. A positive one, I'm sure you'll agree. We're organizing everyone into five-man teams and having them compete to record the highest number of species within a specific amount of time. I think with all the knowledge and experience among you, you will be perfect to join with me."

"You mean, to be on your team?" Dorothy looked like she might burst.

"I thought we were taking a canoe trip," said Rachel. Disappointment edged her question. She had been looking forward to paddling in the swamp.

"Not tomorrow. The conference coordinators have agreed to let me take the group to explore Swamper's Island. Canoe trips will be rescheduled for Saturday and Sunday. But when you hear the rest of the details I'm sure you'll agree it's a positive change."

Swamper's Island. That was the piece of land designated for the land trade.

"*You* will be especially pleased," he said, directing this last bit at Dorothy. "We're going to bag some highly unusual species, trust me. Plus, I'll let you in on a secret — there's a special prize for the team with the most sightings."

"A prize?" said Lark. "What kind of prize?" She flipped her braid over her shoulder, skepticism written all over her face.

"That will all be explained, but everyone gets a free T-shirt, in any case."

Lark made a face.

"If you don't want the prize, you don't have to accept it," said Saxby. "Provided we win." He gave Dorothy's shoulder an extra squeeze, and then turned back to Lark. "If you don't want to participate, I'll try and round up someone else for the team."

"She'll do it," Rachel said promptly.

"Good, very good." Saxby smiled, and moved away.

"What he said about experience," Cecilia said. "I think he was referring to our collective ages. What do you think?"

Lark whirled around to face off with Rachel. "What have you gotten me into this time?"

"I have no idea. Honest." She raised her hands, palms up, fingers spread wide. "You know as much as I do. However, you do realize where we're going tomorrow, don't you?"

"The Okefenokee swamp."

"No! Well yes, but no," said Rachel.

"We're going to Swamper's Island, as in 'land trade' island."

"Oh my." Cecilia's eyes grew wide.

It was clear Lark hadn't realized. "Then maybe we can figure out what's so important about that piece of swampland," she said.

"Right," said Rachel, grabbing hold of Lark's arm. "That's why I opted you in. Because there was no way I wanted Saxby opting you out. The four of us make a pretty good team, not to mention we share the same goal."

"Plus we get free T-shirts." Lark struck a pose.

Cecilia made a tsking noise. "That's not why Dorothy is in."

Rachel shifted uncomfortably and let go of Lark's arm.

Dorothy blushed, ducked her head, and then raised it defiantly. "You know, I kind of like the competitive aspect," she said. "Of course, some of us are going to have to be careful about making things up."

Rachel figured she wasn't referring to Saxby.

CHAPTER 11

At last the line started moving. Filing into the theater, they found seats near the front. The film was incredible. The shots of birds in migration, the sense of flight, combined to leave viewers breathless. Chuck Knapp stood to one side of the screen and talked into a microphone, a black silhouette against his movie. Occasionally he commented on how he'd gotten this or that shot or dropped a nugget of interest about wildlife photography in general. At the end, when the lights came up, he offered to take questions.

Hands shot up throughout the theater.

"Do you shoot your films using digital?" asked a woman near the front.

Knapp swept his hair back from his face. "No, I only use digital for still photographs. For my movies, I prefer shooting with old-fashioned film. There is a quality to film that you don't get with video — a richness in color, a depth, a dimension. Plus, what you shoot is real. It's very easy to manipulate digital images."

"Rumor has it you and Becker found something unusual in the swamp. Can you confirm it?"

Rachel swiveled around to see who had asked the question.

Liam Kelly sat on the edge of his seat.

Had he overheard Becker talking in the Nest, or overheard her conversation with Knapp at lunchtime?

A murmur raced through the crowd.

"That is outside the scope of this discussion," answered Knapp. He seemed uncomfortable, and his gaze swept over the audience.

"Was it the red-cockaded woodpecker, or something else?"

Rachel wondered if, like her, they were all thinking ivory-billed woodpecker.

The crowd refused to let the question rest. "Did you see the actual bird or just foraging signs?" someone else shouted.

"Did you get it on film?"

Knapp stood silent until the audience fell quiet. The tension in the room was palpable. "I will only take questions relating to my film or technique," he stated.

Behind Rachel, a woman said, "He must have gotten it on film. Why else would he be so evasive? I'll bet that's what we'll be seeing on Saturday night."

Knapp pointed to a young man in the front.

"The word is out that you're filming a new TV show about birding. Can you tell us if there's any truth to that?"

Annoyance or discomfort flickered across Knapp's face. He started to open his mouth when Guy Saxby appeared from the opposite side of the audience and took the stage.

"I can address that one," said Saxby. "Can everyone hear me? You, in the back?"

"What the hell —" Knapp pushed forward to center stage.

Satisfied with the crowd's answer, Saxby basked in the spotlight. "I was going to wait and announce this tomorrow night, but since the word is out." He nodded toward the young man, and Rachel wondered if the boy was a plant, possibly one of Saxby's current graduate students. "It's my pleasure to inform you that one of the major networks has picked up my new series, *Extreme Birding*. We're going to be filming the pilot tomorrow."

"What the . . ." Knapp's face turned the shade of sweet beets.

Another murmur rippled through the crowd.

"Film crews will accompany tomorrow's swamp trip into the Okefenokee, where we'll be turning five teams loose on Swamper's Island. The goal will be for each team to list the most birds, *and* the most unusual species, within a specified amount of time."

"What's the prize?" someone shouted.

"Fifty thousand dollars to the winning team, and a matching donation to the birding organization of the winning team's choice."

Rachel's heart started pounding, and she raised her hand to her chest. *Fifty thousand dollars.* Dorothy, Cecilia, and Lark could be counted on to tally up birds, but she was out of her league. My God, what *had* she gotten herself into?

The crowd clapped, as Knapp's voice boomed through the speaker system. "This is not the time or the place, Guy. How many times are you going to pull this sh—"

When he realized he was talking into the mike, he cut himself off and addressed the crowd. "It seems Mr. Saxby has stolen my thunder. I, too, have a televised series in the works."

The crowd "oohed" appreciatively, and Knapp's face brightened. Maybe he figured all was not lost.

"It's a documentary series of exploits in the bird world, called *Avian Adventures*. It's been in the works for a while." Here he shot a pointed look at Saxby. "As we say in the business, the first episode is in the can. The series is expected to air sometime next month."

Knapp looked at Saxby as if daring a response.

Saxby smiled as if he'd gotten an accolade. "Well, you know what they say, great minds think alike."

"My team views this as art, not sport," countered Knapp. Switching off the microphone, he spoke directly to Saxby.

Rachel strained to hear.

Knapp's face had lightened to Bing cherry red, but he still looked mad. His movements were choppy. His voice sounded angry. If only she could make out the words.

In front of her, one woman punched another in the arm and said, "Did you hear that? He has the ivory-billed woodpecker on film!"

"Did he say that?" asked Rachel.

Saxby's voice carried over the crowd. "You're the one who's been scooped, Knapp. My footage will be live, and with plenty of witnesses."

Rachel leaned forward and tapped on the woman's shoulder. "What did Knapp say?"

The woman turned, looking surprised. "He accused Guy Saxby of stealing his idea about the television show, and then he told Saxby if he thought he was going to show this crowd a rare bird it was too bad because he'd been scooped." She paused to listen, and then added, "Saxby said —"

"Thanks." Rachel turned sideways in her seat. The crowd had deteriorated into a jabbering mass.

"Let's go," she whispered to the others, "before this crowd turns into a mob."

Rachel took up the rear, and the four of them pushed their way to the door. The crowd rushed the stage, and Knapp slid back into the shadows. Saxby held court.

"This is great," muttered Lark as they exited the theater. "Just great. We're all going to look like fools on national television. Thanks a lot, Rae."

"Come on, Lark, it's going to be fun," said Dorothy. "We'll be famous, and maybe we'll win some money for Raptor House."

Lark lit up at that.

It had been nearly two years since Rachel had visited the bird rehab center her aunt Miriam had started in Elk Park. She had turned the venture over to the park service, and Eric, Lark's boyfriend, ran the place now. Still, Rachel knew they could use the money.

"That would make Eric happy," said Lark.

"Plus, Guy practically promised we'd see a special bird," continued Dorothy. Excitement raised her voice to high pitch. "I'll bet you dollars to donuts he means the ivory-billed woodpecker."

Rachel filled them in on what the woman in front of her had said. "If she's right, Knapp has it on film. I'll bet that's why Becker changed his mind about the trade."

Dorothy's face fell. "Which completely alters the suspect list."

"But if Knapp has it an film, why not just come out with it?" asked Cecilia.

"Maybe he's waiting until Saturday night," said Lark.

"Or maybe he doesn't have it," said Rachel.

The others looked at her quizzically.

"You heard him say he shoots film," explained Rachel. "He would have to send it out for processing. Any shop on this island would have to ship it out to a lab."

"If that's the case, he won't even know what kind of pictures he has until the film comes back," said Lark. "That would explain his caution. Right now he can't even prove they ever saw the bird."

"I'll bet Guy knows where the bird is," said Dorothy.

They had reached the car, and Rachel stared at her over the top of the rental. Had Saxby confided in her?

"You sound awfully sure," said Lark, voicing Rachel's thoughts.

"He didn't say anything to me, if that's what you're thinking. He just seems so confident that one of the teams will find something great tomorrow, it makes me believe."

"Just because he or Becker or Knapp saw the bird, doesn't mean we will," said Cecilia.

"Unless Guy found a breeding pair," said Lark.

Rachel's eyes never left Dorothy. If Saxby had told her as much, she didn't react.

"If they're nesting," Lark continued, "they'll stay in the same area. Of course, I have no idea what their range is."

A lightbulb went off in Rachel's head. "You realize that either way, regardless of where Becker stood on the trade, if there's an endangered bird on their land, the Andersons' chances of selling goes right out the window. It becomes the land trade or nothing."

"Which plays in their favor for a land swap," said Lark. "The developers would have to jump through legal hoops to ensure that they aren't harming any endangered species, or to at least prove they are rebuilding any habitat they do harm, and the state would really want control of the land."

"I wonder what it means for the Carters?" mused Rachel. So far they hadn't eliminated any suspects from their list, except for Beau and Reggie. If there was an endangered species living on Swamper's Island, would the state need the Carters' land for access? The original plan was to build a visitor's center on the Carters' acreage, or provide the developers access.

Rachel knew one thing for certain: The more she learned, the more she was convinced that Becker's murder had something to do with turf.

Upon reaching their suite, Lark jumped into the shower and Rachel logged on to the Internet. She checked for a message from Kirk and came up emptyhanded. At least she had something to tell him:

The plot thickens. Guy Saxby's secret is out. He signed with a major network to do a reality-based TV show called "Extreme Birding." The first episode stars yours truly. Filming commences tomorrow. I trust this is what you were looking for? But there's more. Chuck Knapp has a competing program called "Avian Adventures." It appears he and Becker discovered another ivory-billed woodpecker. Don't you wish you were here? I do.

She paused, and then added:

Love, Rachel

With a few mouse clicks, she sent the message and opened to the Web page discussing the stealing of Becker's ideas. As she'd suspected, Saxby was named as the culprit. There was no proof, only Becker's rantings and his threats to sue.

But he hadn't. Nor, apparently, had he worked with Saxby on anything since.

Rachel suspected they might have been working at cross-purposes on the same project. Or Becker might actively have been out to get Saxby fired. Either one of those could provide Saxby with a motive for killing Becker, albeit a pretty lame one. If it was true that Saxby had stolen Becker's research, Rachel could see why Becker might have wanted to kill his department head, but Saxby had already weathered the accusations of his graduate student. And if the ivory-billed woodpecker was on Swamper's Island, Saxby would have his footage tomorrow, and his coup d'état.

Dorothy would be happy to learn Saxby appeared to be in the clear. Less happy to hear how many people believed he had plagiarized his book. Still, it was only hearsay.

Now I'm making excuses for him.

Regardless, Dorothy needed to know, Rachel decided. She knocked on the door connecting their suites, and then opened it. Cecilia sat on one bed reading. Dorothy was nowhere to be seen.

"Where is she?" asked Rachel, nodding toward Dorothy's bed.

Cecilia dropped her reading glasses onto her chest. "I thought she was in your room. Of all the sneaky . . . She must have gone out."

"She wouldn't have gone alone," said Rachel, keeping her voice steady while her mind was racing.

"Sure she would have. She's in love. She's like a teenager." Cecilia paused to let the meaning sink in. "Oh my, I think we ought to mount a search party." She slid out of bed in one smooth motion, pulled on a pair of blue pedal pushers, and tucked in her blue nightshirt. Then she reconsidered and pulled it out. The result looked strangely fashionable — probably because the two items were an identical shade of blue.

Rachel hovered between amusement and alarm.

Then the door clicked, opened, and Dorothy peered around the edge of it.

"Good, you're awake," she said, waving a handful of papers. "Look what I've got. Releases! All we have to do is sign these and we're in like Flynn!"

"What are you talking about?" Cecilia crossed her arms and sat down hard on her bed. "You had us worried to death."

"We have to sign these to appear on television," replied Dorothy, ignoring her sister's admonishment. "There are only three camera teams, and one will be with us all the way."

Rachel's heart sank. *Extreme Birding* carried too much pressure. All she wanted to do was relax and enjoy the scenery, especially now that she knew Saxby's big secret. They could leave it to the police to figure out who murdered Becker. It didn't affect them now.

"And guess who the other teams are that will have camera crews? Some really big names! But we'll have Guy," she added confidently.

Rachel's mouth went dry. "Guy's competing?"

"Of course, he's the ultimate extreme birder."

"Dorothy, I have to tell you something about Guy." Without waiting to see her reaction, Rachel forged ahead. "I went back on that message board on my computer. The department head who stole Becker's research . . . it was Guy."

Dorothy's face contorted into an angry mask.

"The good news is I didn't find any reason that Guy would want to kill Becker. But Becker sure had it in for Guy. It was the same story I got from Sonja Becker."

"Posh thus, as my mother used to say," said Dorothy.

Cecilia frowned. "I don't recall her ever saying that."

Dorothy ignored her. "You know how things are. Younger teaching assistants are used as research associates all of the time. That's how one learns the ropes. In that job, you have to expect that your advisors are going to use your findings in their own publications. It's part of academia."

Rachel started to argue, but maybe she

had it wrong. At any rate, no doubt Dorothy would be impossible to convince.

Proving Rachel correct, Dorothy charged on. "Think of all the things Guy Saxby's done in his career." She waved the release forms in the air. "He can talk about anything bird-related. Does he sound like somebody who had to steal someone else's research to publish?"

When neither of them answered, she answered for them. "No. Becker was jealous, that's all."

"Maybe," said Rachel.

"Oh my, she has love blinders on."

Dorothy faltered. "It doesn't matter. Guy has promised that we'll be on camera tomorrow. We are going to win that money for Raptor House. You'll see that you're wrong about him. He is going to prove his mettle." She handed Rachel two releases. "Here's one for you, and one for Lark. Now we should all get to bed so we can be extra sharp tomorrow."

Cecilia scoffed. "Or so somebody can get her much-needed beauty sleep."

CHAPTER 12

Rachel didn't. She tried to sleep, but she tossed and turned, and then finally got up. The clock dial read eleven p.m. They had to be up in six hours.

Lark snored softly in the next bed, so Rachel pulled on her shorts in a beam of moonlight, and then headed downstairs in search of hot chocolate. A small coffee bar had been tucked into a corner for guests, and Rachel helped herself to a packet of Swiss Miss. Three carafes labeled decaf, coffee, and water sat next to the tray of mugs. Dumping the chocolate into the mug, she pushed the pump on the water, and the carafe sputtered. She pushed again, and it spit a burble of water before it finally gave up.

Darn.

There was no clerk at the desk, so Rachel picked up the carafe and ducked her head into the bar. There was no bartender either.

Who needed staff with all the birders in bed?

The dining room was closed, but yellow light leaked out from beneath the swinging doors into the kitchen. Maybe she could find someone in there.

Pushing open the swinging door, she stepped into a large room with metal counters and racks. A dishwasher crammed full of dinner dishes churned in the corner, its water spray visible. A woman's voice screeched from deeper inside.

"What the hell is wrong with you?"

Rachel stopped in mid-stride. It sounded like Patricia Anderson. Was she talking to her?

Rachel's free hand flew to her chest, and she peered around the corner of the nearest dish rack. Patricia stood sideways, center aisle, her hands on her hips. A snarl marred her lips. "You are seventeen years old."

I'm in the clear. Rachel leaned farther around the dish rack. Katie Anderson stood facing her mother. Her black hair was pulled up in a ponytail, and she wore a thin, low-cut tank top, which pushed out in a small bump over her low-rise jeans. Her hands flew to her face, and she rubbed one of her eyes.

The little-girl gesture in a woman's body touched Rachel's heart. There was something about the way the girl acted that reminded Rachel of herself not so long ago. There had been times, during her divorce, that she had felt so vulnerable she had wanted to curl up in the fetal position and die. Watching Katie, Rachel sensed the same despair.

"How could you be so stupid?"

Tears spilled over and tumbled down Katie's face. She snatched up a tissue and blotted her eyes. "I'm not stupid."

"Wait until your father gets back from Brunswick and I tell him what you've been up to. What could you possibly think you'd achieve by visiting Sonja Becker? How could you possibly think she would welcome you and your bastard child with open arms?"

Katie was pregnant? With Paul Becker's child? Sonja Becker said her husband cheated, and that he liked them young.

"This baby is entitled to a decent upbringing. I expected she might help us. It was worth a try. It's better than I can expect from you."

"Why you little . . ." Patricia raised her hand as though to strike Katie, and then changed her mind, balling her hand into a fist by her side. "Your daddy and I plan to see this child placed in a loving home. In the meantime, you better pray this land trade goes through so we have the money to pay for it."

Did that mean the developer had backed out?

"I'm not giving up my baby." Katie, the young woman-child, stood her ground. "That's why I went to see Mrs. Becker. I figured she might understand."

The theme song from *The Graduate* started playing in Rachel's head.

Katie's voice rose in timbre. "You and Daddy can't tell me what to do with my baby." Her hand gently stroked her belly. "Now get out of my way. I'm leaving."

With that, Katie pushed past her mother and headed in Rachel's direction. Rachel drew back against the dish rack. If she tried to leave, Katie would see her. If she stepped into the open it would be obvious she was eavesdropping. Where could she hide?

"Katie Jo Anderson, you get back here," ordered Patricia.

Rachel heard Katie stop. Had she turned back around? If that was the case, Patricia would be the one facing the door.

Patricia's voice edged toward hysterical. "You do understand that we're ruined if the land trade doesn't go through."

"That has nothing to do with me. I'm not

the one who overextended myself buying this stupid hotel."

She heard Patricia draw a ragged breath.

"Katie Jo, we need your help," she said, her voice softened. "Did Sonja Becker admit there was a film?"

Rachel felt her stomach twist. Did this woman have no scruples? Was she going to use her pregnant daughter to try and get her hands on the film?

"Yeah." Katie sounded petulant. Rachel could see her stance through the dish rack, her arms crossed tightly across the tip of her abdomen, one knee cocked.

"Daddy and I need it, honey. That's the only proof that the bird exists. If that film is made public, the developer will back out, and the state can force us to protect the swampland. There will be no reason for them to trade acreages. We'll be ruined."

Katie didn't respond.

Rachel listened carefully for footsteps.

"Katie Jo, did Sonja tell you where it was?"

"You disgust me, Mother. All you've ever cared about is money and status."

"Please, Katie Jo."

"She told me to ask Chuck Knapp. He's the one who shot the footage."

Realizing their conversation was coming to an end, Rachel took the cue. Kicking the

197

door open, she swung the empty carafe and acted like she was just walking in. "I thought I heard voices."

Patricia's face hardened into a smile. Katie looked down at the ground, and then brushed past Rachel and disappeared through the swinging doors.

Rachel held up the carafe. "You're out of water."

Drinking hot chocolate on the screened-in porch, Rachel breathed a sigh of relief. Thank heavens neither of them had questioned her entrance. Patricia had filled the carafe, and then excused herself to do some work in her office. Katie was gone, and the desk clerk was back with a friendly smile.

Now, listening to the sounds of the cicadas and to the surf gently pounding the sand, Rachel tried to relax. A small noise startled her, and she couldn't shake the impression that someone watched her from the shadows of the magnolia trees. Her mind flashed to the golf course, and then conjured an image of Trula, the voodoo lady. *Oona mus tek cyear.*

Rachel shivered and pushed out of the chair. Setting the cup on the service table, she nodded to the desk clerk and climbed the stairs to her room. The old floorboards creaked underneath the carpet, and she imagined old Harry frowning down from his portrait.

Opening her hotel room door, she knocked a piece of paper along the floor. Bending down, she picked it up. Large black letters in block print spelled out:

QUIT SNOOPING OR DIE.

Rachel froze in place. Her whole body tingled. Whipping around, she searched the landing for a sign of anyone in the hallway or on the stairs. Stepping into her room, she slammed the door, turned the deadbolt, and drew the chain.

Lark sat bolt upright in bed. "Rachel? What's wrong?"

Rachel flipped on the light.

Lark blinked in bed like a great-horned owl. Rachel thrust the note into her hand. Lark blanched.

"Where did you get this?"

"I found it on the floor. Someone must have shoved it under the door." She told Lark about her trip downstairs for hot chocolate, the conversation she'd overheard, and about feeling someone watching her.

"We need to call the police," said Lark.

Rachel agreed.

Detective Stone arrived within twenty minutes. By then Dorothy and Cecilia were up as well, disturbed by the urgent whispering of the occupants of their adjoining suite.

"Tell me again," the detective said.

This time she gladly repeated her story. The detective sat rigid in the chair by the window, while his partner leaned against the doorjamb scribbling notes. The detective held the now-sheathed warning by a corner.

"We have a suspect list if you want it," said Dorothy.

Detective Stone rolled his eyes. "Sure, give it to my partner. Meanwhile, I'll check this paper for fingerprints." He didn't sound optimistic. "Only the two of you touched it?"

Cecilia raised her hand. "I might have touched it, too, Detective."

"That figures." He stood up shaking his head. "Ms. Wilder, Ms. Drummond, and you." He pointed two fingers and included both sisters. "I want you all to steer clear of my investigation from here on out. No more developing suspect lists, no more eavesdropping. *Do you understand?*" He shook his head. "It nearly got you killed this afternoon. Let me and my men handle these matters. Is that understood?"

200

"Got it," said Rachel.

Lark and Cecilia nodded.

Dorothy just narrowed her eyes.

The alarm went off a few hours later. The women grabbed coffee and bagels on the way out the door, and the four of them made the bus with time to spare. Rachel was a bit surprised that it wasn't the colorful Okefenokee Swamp Tours bus they'd ridden on before.

"There's been a change," was all Saxby offered.

The ride took an hour. Dorothy sat smugly beside Saxby the entire way. Cecilia sat two seats behind, craning her neck around camera equipment to keep an eye on her sister. Rachel and Lark sat on the other side of the bus and enjoyed an excellent view of Saxby showing Dorothy points of interest.

"I admit it," said Lark. "I don't see what she sees in him. To me, he seems kind of smitten with himself. What in the heck do you suppose is going on?"

"Chemistry," said Rachel.

"I disagree. I think he's using her."

"For what?" There certainly wasn't anything physical going on between them unless she was drugging Cecilia to sneak out at night. For that matter, Cecilia might be a heavy sleeper. Saxby's room *was* right above them.

The thought chilled her. Then another thought crept in behind it. *Could he have been the one who slipped her the note?*

"Besides, what does it matter?" asked Rachel. "She's enjoying the attention, and she has lots of keepers." Rachel gestured at Cecilia. "She seems happy. What harm can there be in a mild flirtation? The three of you are headed back to Colorado in a couple of days, and that will be the end of it."

Lark looked skeptical. "Did you see the way she forced me to sign that release? Not only are we going to humiliate ourselves on national television, we consented to it."

"If the pilot doesn't work for the network, maybe he can sell it to *America's Funniest Home Videos*."

"Don't even joke, Rae." Moments later, Lark's head turned. "Did you see that sign? DON'T FEED THE ALLIGATORS. Who on earth would stop and feed the alligators?"

"I don't know. They have those signs on ski lifts, too. DON'T JUMP OFF THE SKI LIFT. Same thing. Who in their right mind would jump?"

"I guess some people think alligators are

cute," conceded Lark.

"Well I think bears are cute," said Rachel, "but that doesn't mean I'd want to be one's lunch."

The driver braked suddenly, and Lark grabbed the back of the seat. "What's going on?"

Rachel thought of an alligator crossing.

The bus slowed, pulled into a makeshift parking area behind another bus, and both vehicles sat there spewing fumes.

"We don't seem to be there yet," Lark observed.

Rachel noticed that on the other side of the bus, the cameraman sitting near Cecilia had started filming out the window. "I think the view is on the other side."

Both of them moved forward and squeezed into the seat next to Cecilia. Through the window, they saw a line of protesters blocking the road.

"There's Fancy Carter with her pet alligator," said Lark. "Rhinestones and all."

"You're kidding." Rachel craned to see.

"Yes," Lark said. "About the alligator."

Rachel had to agree, Fancy did look like the sort of person who would have a pet alligator, and she glittered on the front line, flanked by both of her sons. No wonder they had taken a different bus this morning.

"There's Nevin Anderson," said Lark. "I wonder what the heck is going on?"

Rachel waited for Lark to make some sharp observation about him, too, but it didn't come.

"Liam Kelly's here," said Rachel, standing up to get a look at Dorothy and Guy. Saxby didn't look happy, but Dorothy did. Rachel flashed Dorothy a signal, and she gave Rachel a thumbs-up.

"What's happening?" mouthed Rachel.

Dorothy shrugged.

Saxby turned to the bus driver. A minute later the door opened, and the two men strode across the road to the protestors. Rachel followed them off the bus.

"Get back in your rig," said Dwayne Carter. He noticed Rachel, smiled, and winked. "You can stay."

Guy Saxby glanced over his shoulder and glared. "Get back in the bus, Rachel."

"I want to know what's going on just as much as you do. This is our field trip."

Saxby turned back to the crowd. "I insist you move out of the way."

Lark appeared at Rachel's shoulder. "Do you think this is staged? Our first obstacle — get past the swamp people."

Now there was an idea, thought Rachel, except Saxby didn't seem to be taking this in stride.

"The cameras *are* rolling," she said.

"This is our land, Saxby," said Fancy. "If you want access to the Okefenokee, you can make it down the road."

"You know this is the only quick access to Swamper's Island. The only other way is by boat."

"And you still need permission to land," said Nevin Anderson, stepping forward. "I don't remember agreeing to let you on my island."

Rachel wondered if Fancy would allow Nevin Anderson access? She controlled the gateway, and as long as all deals were on the table, she was sitting pretty. What happened if all deals were off?

"There's a right-of-way easement into the swamp," said Saxby. "You have to let us through."

By now the bus had emptied, and the two camps faced off. Actually, three camps. Rachel noticed that Liam Kelly and his protestors seemed to have their own agenda. The group carried signs that read STOP THE LAND TRADE, STOP ALL DEVELOPMENT, and LET THE SWAMP GO WILD.

"No land swap," they chanted. "Let the swamp go wild."

Saxby pointed toward Liam. "I'm on your side."

"You're exploiting the birds," Liam yelled back. "You're no better than the others."

Saxby appealed to Dwayne Carter. "Be reasonable. This television show can put your swamp tour business on the map."

"You want access?" countered Dwayne. "The public right-of-way is the next turn down the highway. It takes you to the public dock. From there, you can access the swamp, provided you have your own boats."

Rachel noticed Dwight edge toward a battered old truck. A rifle hung in the gun rack in the back window, and his hand clamped down on the stock. A stab of fear caused her stomach muscles to clench.

"Guy." She tugged on Saxby's shirt. "I think we should leave and sort this out later."

"Do you have any idea what it costs to pay these film crews?" he bellowed to no one in particular.

Dwight freed the rifle and drew it out the window. Rachel wondered if the detective should check its ballistics.

Raising the barrel toward the sky, Dwight cocked the rifle and fired.

The shot quieted the crowd.

Dwight cradled the rifle, and advanced on

Saxby. "You are trespassing here, and I am ordering you off my land. If you don't skedaddle in the next five minutes, I'm going to put a bullet in your ass."

Saxby's eyes widened, and Rachel noticed his hands shook. "Back on the bus," she said to Lark. "Come on, Cecilia and Dorothy."

Dorothy started to step up beside Saxby, but Cecilia grabbed her arm. "Dorothy MacBean, you get back on that bus. I'm not going to have my sister shot defending a pompous . . . a man like Guy Saxby."

"What did you call him?" Dorothy whirled on Cecilia, and Rachel took the opportunity to push Dorothy toward the bus.

"How dare you?" Dorothy continued. "You just don't understand him. You're just jealous." Her voice lacked conviction, however, and she did what the others told her to do.

Saxby tried talking with Nevin Anderson, but from Saxby's body language, Rachel could tell he was losing. Moments later he said something sharp to the cameraman and strode back to the bus. The driver followed him aboard, made a slow, arduous turn with the bus, and headed back.

As they picked up speed, Saxby stood up and spoke into the microphone. "This is not our day, folks. But, trust me, we will be

207

back. I'm sorry to disappoint you." Then he sat back down, this time next to the cameraman.

Dorothy sat with Rachel. "It was just a case of ruffled feathers."

Rachel lifted her hair off her neck. The air conditioning had gone off while the bus had been stopped, and she was feeling a little ruffled herself. "This isn't going to make such a great pilot."

"Guy thinks Chuck Knapp put the protestors up to this," said Dorothy. "At least that's what he said when we first pulled up. I'll bet he's right. It's a pretty cutthroat world, this extreme birding."

"Still," said Rachel. "He's not going to have much to show at the keynote. It's apt to be pretty boring."

CHAPTER 13

What the keynote lacked in extreme birding footage, it made up for in drama.

Rachel watched Saxby work the crowd. He was an engaging speaker who used his charm to involve the audience, and he clearly knew his stuff. To make up for the lack of raw footage from the day, he showed clips from a trip he had made to Africa and sprinkled in lots of commentary: how he avoided the oversafaried African hot spots and detailing the effects of tourism on the canopy, on the animals, and on the natives, pointing out what his own party did to minimize their impact on the environment.

Comparing his film with Knapp's, Rachel decided the biggest contrast was Saxby didn't have the amazing shots of the birds. A typical shot in Saxby's film showed him or one of his group pointing at a bird, followed by a zoomed-in close-up. Knapp's film had recorded the birds without their awareness. Knapp apparently had patience, something Saxby sorely lacked.

The lights came up, and Saxby moved from stage left to center stage, with a comfortable motion that indicated he knew he belonged there.

"Questions? You, sir." Saxby held up his hand to shield his eyes and gazed toward the back of the auditorium. Then, just as quickly, he shifted his gaze to the opposite side and pointed to a woman. "Ma'am."

"You can't dodge my questions that easily," shouted the man from the back.

Rachel turned and recognized Knapp. At the moment he didn't look very patient at all.

"I want to know what the hell you think you're doing, stealing my film!"

"Oh my, who is that?" Cecilia wanted to know, craning around in her chair.

"Chuck Knapp," whispered Rachel.

"What is he saying?" asked Lark.

The murmur from the audience drowned out Dorothy's reaction, but the crowd quieted when Saxby replied.

"The question, in case everybody didn't hear it, was why did I steal Mr. Knapp's film?"

Rachel skin prickled. Knapp's film was missing. He had to be talking about the footage from Swamper's Island.

"Chuck, what the hell are you talking about? This footage was clearly my vision, my group, taken on my cameras —"

"I'm not talking about your stupid safari film," hollered Knapp, heading up the aisle toward the stage.

Rachel wondered if somebody ought to stop him.

"I'm talking about my more recent footage, which someone has misappropriated."

Where had it disappeared from?

"We all know how you have done this kind of thing before." Knapp advanced down the aisle.

Saxby looked indignant. "If your film has disappeared, I suggest you take it up with the authorities rather than blame an innocent person. Or perhaps you should keep better track of your property."

Knapp made a guttural noise. "Don't think you can get away with this. I had better not see my footage used in your so-called reality show."

"Now that would be pretty stupid of me, wouldn't it, Chuck? You may have prevented me from getting my own footage today, but I assure you I'm capable of coming through for my producers without resorting to theft."

"Do you really expect anyone to believe

that? Considering your history?"

Rachel glanced at Dorothy. Her face was the color of milk.

Knapp stood on the floor below Saxby, but kept his volume high. "You have stolen careers with your plagiarism. Well, you are not stealing mine!"

Saxby glared down at him. "That's a fairly serious accusation, Chuck."

"A leopard cannot change its spots. You may have changed your modus operandi, but you are still a thief."

Saxby spoke into the microphone. "Is that proof according to Knapp?"

The filmmaker exploded. "You specialize in the kind of theft where nothing is missing. You steal property no one can ever recover. But film is tangible, and you damn well know what I'm talking about."

Saxby looked over Knapp's head, out into the audience, officially dismissing him. "The lady in the back there. Miss? Do you have a question?"

Over the buzz of the audience, the woman shouted out something to the effect that wouldn't TV shows like the one Saxby proposed attract hordes of tourists to converge on delicate ecosystems? But Knapp refused to let the show go on. He grabbed the cord of the microphone and yanked on it.

Did he intend to vault himself up onto the stage?

Saxby released the microphone and Knapp fell backwards, to gasps from the audience. The microphone clattered to the stage.

"Why doesn't somebody do something?" Dorothy hissed. "We could do something. We could go up there and . . ."

Knapp was yelling now, but he couldn't be understood over the crowd. Saxby's voice carried without the benefit of the microphone.

"Apparently Mr. Knapp is upset because he has nothing to present tomorrow night for his segment of the program," said Saxby. "And instead of working up something, he came here, and chose to disrupt tonight's program. Is there any security in the building?"

Two maroon-clad security guards hustled down the aisle.

"Now, ma'am, to address your question . . ."

"I don't think Saxby needs our help, Dorothy," said Lark. "He seems to be doing well enough on his own."

But Knapp refused to be muffled. He

clambered to his feet, and then hoisted himself onto the stage. "You will pay for this."

Was he threatening Saxby?

"Really, Chuck, this is unprofessional," said Saxby, taking a step back while the security guards tried dragging Knapp from the stage. "If you had availed yourself of modern technology — I'm talking digital, Chuck — then maybe this wouldn't have happened."

"I wish Kirk were here to see this," Rachel said to nobody in particular. "Assaults, allegations —"

"Unfounded allegations," Dorothy muttered.

"Un*proven,* anyway," said Lark.

Dorothy threw daggers at Lark with her eyes.

Evan Kearns took the stage, looking very stern. The audience appeared to be holding its breath to see if Knapp was going to take a punch at Saxby. Saxby, prudently enough, took another step back.

"Gentlemen," Evan said. "This is not what any of us came to see. Now, if you wish to continue this discussion, I suggest you do so in private?" He gave Knapp a hard look. "Chuck, this is Saxby's stage. You get to speak tomorrow night."

The men faced off, then Knapp drew a breath so deep that the microphone picked it up. Knapp stalked off through the wings. Saxby bent down, picked up the mike, and without looking or sounding the least bit ruffled, continued.

"To address the question about whether shows such as mine would cause tourists to converge thus creating an unfavorable impact on areas with delicate ecologies, I don't believe that will happen. To a small portion of the population these are already areas of interest, but the cost involved in undertaking expeditions into these areas can be quite prohibitive for the average person. In fact, it's with that in mind that we present this programming. We want to share the experience with people who have neither the time nor the funds, but who desperately want to experience and learn about diverse ecosystems and their denizens.

"Now, if you'll forgive me for not tackling any more questions, I thank you for your attention."

He paused a moment for applause, which came in a few scattered bursts.

"In other words," he added, "the show's over. It's time to hit the bar."

This got a few laughs, and another buzz of confusion.

"The bar sounds like a good idea," said Lark. "That was the darnedest thing I've ever seen."

"That horrid man making those accusations about Guy," said Dorothy.

Rachel started to speak, but Dorothy held up her hand. "I know what you're going to say, but I still don't believe a word of it. He's a decent man."

The other three stood in momentary silence, and Rachel became suddenly aware of the crowd milling around them. She saw Wolcott talking with Nevin Anderson, Sonja sitting with Liam Kelly, and Dwayne Carter winked at her from the back of the auditorium. She remembered his brother's rifle. Someone had taken a shot at Chuck Knapp today with a long-barreled gun, and had narrowly missed hitting her. She wondered where the Carters had been around noon.

"I think we should talk about this back in our suite," said Rachel, feeling suddenly uncomfortable in the crowd.

Lark nodded.

"Well I for one would *love* to go on the kind of expedition Saxby was talking about," Cecilia chirped. "I have the time, and the money —"

Dorothy cut her off. "Let's go. I'm supposed to meet Guy in the hotel bar."

"Oh my, do you think that's wise, Dot? After the scene here tonight . . ."

"He'll need my support more than ever. Besides, it's a public place, and I'm certainly old enough to meet a man for a drink."

"I say go," said Rachel, a plan formulating in her mind. If Saxby had stolen the film there was only one place it could be — in his hotel room. "I'll help you find him."

"As usual," mumbled Cecilia.

Rachel pulled Lark aside on the way to the car. "I have an idea."

"Why do I not like the sound of this?"

"We're going to need Cecilia's help, too."

"This doesn't involve rock climbing, does it?"

Rachel understood her hesitation. The last time she'd had an idea Lark had ended up swinging off a rope with a broken ankle. "No, nothing like that."

"Going for a midnight swim in the swamp? How about feeding alligators?"

"I told you, I'm not that crazy."

"Let's hear it then."

"If Saxby has the film, it has to be in his room. We just need to make sure Dorothy keeps him occupied in the bar for half an hour, while we get in and out of his room."

"You are nuts."

"It's the only way to be sure. It's the only

place he could have it."

"He might have destroyed it already."

"Would you destroy a film that has the only clear shot of an ivory-billed woodpecker taken since the 1940s?"

"No." Lark twisted her braid. "Why don't we call the police and let them investigate?"

"They need just cause to enter his room. He could move the film by the time they obtained a warrant." Rachel could see by Lark's expression she was cracking. "If we find the film, we'll call Detective Stone."

"Do you think Saxby's the one who slipped the note under our door?"

Rachel had considered that. She bet Dorothy was keeping him apprised of their investigation. "I think it's possible he was the one shooting at Knapp —"

"Or you."

"Or me out on the golf course," finished Rachel.

"Are you two coming?" called Dorothy. She drummed her fingers on the hood of the car.

Lark kept Dorothy talking in the front seat while Rachel whispered the plan to Cecilia in the back.

"Oh my, I don't like this."

"Like what?" asked Dorothy.

"Shhhh," said Rachel. "She doesn't like

what's happening with Saxby and Knapp."

"Neither do I." Dorothy started to go on, and Rachel turned back to face Cecilia.

"It's simple. All you have to do is make sure Dorothy and Saxby stay in the bar for at least a half hour." Rachel knew how gutsy Cecilia could be. She'd come through more than once, risking her own life to help save Rachel and her aunt. "It's easy duty."

"Easy for you to say."

Rachel wondered how hard it was for Cecilia to see Dorothy so smitten. It's what she had always wanted for her sister, but now that it had happened, was she jealous? Or was she just afraid for her sister, falling in love with someone the likes of Guy Saxby?

"Fine, I'll do it."

They stayed in the bar long enough to make sure Dorothy and Saxby made contact. Saxby draped a proprietary arm around Dorothy's shoulders. Dorothy glowed, and even Saxby looked pretty content. Cecilia, on the other side of Saxby, looked wistful.

"He's a take-charge kind of person," said Rachel. "I can see the attraction." She thought of her ex. "Men like to reel you in. They're great for the short term, it's the long haul that becomes a problem."

"Who's talking about the long haul?" said Lark. "You don't think Dorothy and Saxby will continue to see each other?"

Rachel shrugged. As much as she hated to admit it, they made a cute couple.

Lark yawned. "I think I'm going to head upstairs."

"Me, too," said Rachel. She winked at Cecilia, who perked up in her chair.

"Maybe we should all go up," said Dorothy, patting Saxby's hand. "You must be exhausted after your ordeal."

"No," said Cecilia. "I want another drink."

Dorothy looked at her sister, surprise widening her eyes. "You rarely have one."

Saxby chuckled. "If she wants another, she can have another." He raised his hand to catch Patricia Anderson's eye. "I don't mind sitting here with you and keeping her company."

Rachel noticed him squeeze Dorothy's shoulder. She settled into the crook of his arm. "Fine, then."

So far, so good. Rachel and Lark said their goodnights, and hurried upstairs to their room. *Drink slowly, Cecilia.*

Rachel pulled off her socks and shoes, rolled her pants up to her knees, then slipped on a hotel bathrobe and cinched it tight around her waist. Heading to the shower, she ducked her head in and flipped on the faucet.

"Look, I know my way around hotels," said Lark. "I'm sure there's a better way to do this."

"How?" asked Rachel, barefoot, with her hair wet as if she'd just shampooed. "Patricia introduced you to the hotel staff. They know who you are. They don't know me."

"Most of them know that you're my roommate. Besides, how sure are you about the room number?"

"It's the suite right above ours," Rachel said. "Remember when Saxby checked in? The clerk told him third floor, west wing, first room on the left."

Lark looked like she might start crying at any minute. Rachel, on the other hand, was brimming with adrenaline. "It's going to be okay," she said. "Just stay here. I'll call you once I get in the room."

"What if you run into someone we know?"

"No one knows what floor we're on. Cecilia will keep Saxby and Dorothy in the bar. We're wasting time."

"If security's any good, they're going to ask you for ID."

Rachel held her hands out. "Obviously, I don't have any. It's inside the room."

Lark let her breath out with a *pfft.*

"If I get caught, well then, oops, I had too much to drink. I'm on the wrong floor."

"In your bathrobe. With wet hair. I mean, honestly, Rae — you don't look old enough to have Alzheimer's."

Rachel gave her two thumbs-up, opened the door, and peered down the corridor. "All clear."

She stuck her head out and listened. There was no noise coming from the elevator, and no one coming up the stairs. Slipping through the door, she zipped across the hall and took the steps to the third floor two at a time.

She made it without seeing anyone, but her heart pounded. It was amazing what the thought of mischief did to an ordinary trek up a flight of stairs.

Like on her floor, an antique table stood in the center of the hall. It bore a floral arrangement, several complimentary bottles of water, and a telephone. Rachel gazed down the hall and saw what she needed — dinner trays sitting on the floor.

The elevator *ding*ed, and Rachel ducked into the indentation behind the stairway. She barely picked up the sounds of conversation above the thudding of her heart. The voices receded, and she leaned out, watching with one eye as a woman unlocked her door while another one talked. They were discussing Saxby's fiasco of a keynote speech.

As soon as the women had shut their door behind them, Rachel started back down the hall. Stopping in front of Saxby's room, she double-checked the room number. For a second she was seized by panic. What if this room hadn't suited him either, and he'd asked for a change?

Get a grip, Wilder. He would have told Dorothy.

As quietly as possible she picked up the discarded dinner tray closest to Saxby's room, set it down just outside the door, and then slid it sideways. If she were really doing this, and had locked herself out, which way would she have slid it?

Then the worst happened. The next door down opened, and a man stuck his head out, looking almost as furtive as Rachel felt. She turned toward Saxby's door and grabbed the handle, realizing at the same moment that the tray she had stolen was, in all likelihood, his.

Just great. She looked like she was stealing the remains of his dinner.

The man, losing his furtive air, walked toward the elevator, shooting a glance back at her.

Okay, she'd been made. This plan wasn't working.

Resolving to slink back to her room and hope the guy didn't think anything strange about it, she turned toward the stairs. She could explain her appearance by saying she'd been at the hotel's spa, gone to the wrong floor . . . That was a good story. Now she only had to remember not to just spill it, but only to volunteer it if asked.

"Excuse me, do you need something?"

Rachel whipped around. Furtive Man was back, apparently having decided that a wild-looking woman in a bathrobe was more interesting than whatever he'd been heading for.

"Oh. I . . ." She stopped. He'd seen her adjusting the tray. She had to go back to her original story — that she'd put her tray out in the hall and that the door had closed behind her — except that would draw his attention to the fact that she'd stolen *his* tray.

"You need a maid," he said brusquely. "Hang on, I'll see if I can find one and send her your way." Juggling two cans of soda, he inserted his card into the slot on his door.

Rachel shivered. "Thanks."

Just what she didn't need — a helpful sort. He'd probably stand with her until help arrived. Lark had been right. This *was* a stupid idea.

Once the man disappeared into his room, she headed for the stairs, speeding up when she heard the elevator *ding* again. There was no point in letting the entire hotel see her with her hair wet and going frizzy, not to mention herself in a state of dishabille.

"Oh, miss?"

She turned. A uniformed maid had spoken and was making her way toward Rachel. Either Furtive Man had located a maid very quickly, or this was some kind of sting operation.

Think fast, Wilder! "I was looking for a phone."

"No problem," the maid said. "This one?" She indicated the room Furtive Man had come out of.

Rachel pointed at Saxby's room.

The maid nodded and inserted her key.

Rachel couldn't speak. Thoughts flitted through her mind. Maybe Saxby had a hidden secret roommate. Or maybe she did have it wrong and this wasn't his room.

The maid flung the door open and Rachel stepped inside, trying to look relieved instead of anxious. "I feel so stupid," she said. *True enough.*

"Oh, this happens all the time," replied

the maid. "At least you were wearing something. Don't give it another thought."

"Same to you," Rachel said. "I mean — thanks." Rachel realized the maid probably wanted a tip, but she'd forgotten to think of that.

CHAPTER 14

Once the maid walked away, Rachel shut the door, pressed her forehead to the wood, and stared for a moment at the directions for escape in case of a fire posted on the back of the door.

Get moving, Wilder.

The first thing she did was head for the phone and call Lark. "I'm in."

"I'll keep a look out."

Rachel hung up the phone and moved to the center of the room. One lamp was on, shedding totally inadequate light around the suite. Her first decision was not to flip on the overhead, just in case.

In case of what? In case someone was watching through the window? Fortunately the curtains were already drawn.

The bedside table had a marked-up Hyde Island Birding and Nature Festival schedule on it, identifying the room's occupant as someone attending the conference. That was a start. A stack of signed release forms for *Extreme Birding* on the TV console confirmed it was Saxby's room.

The most efficient way to search would be to start around the room clockwise, and then keep going until she either found something or got back to her starting point. She moved back to the door, and started with the closet. She searched silently and quickly, resolving not to be distracted by any notable things she discovered that didn't pertain directly to the missing film. She figured the film reel had to be at least four inches in diameter.

She checked inside his brown wing tips and hiking boots to see if anything was concealed in the heels, went through his pockets and thought she had something right off the bat — it turned out to be a Frank Sinatra CD. At least Saxby had good taste in music. A 35mm film canister turned out to hold safety pins.

Once through the closet she moved clockwise through the bathroom, finding only the usual stuff in rather a messy array. Shaving lotion, underwear on the floor that made her wish she were wearing gloves, Bay Rum aftershave, Clinique for Men, now that was interesting. Interesting, but not relevant.

On the table she found piles of papers —

a manuscript, a contract for the TV series, some pages printed from the Internet. Things indicative of plagiarism, or not. Things that might interest Kirk, or not. The pile would no doubt make fascinating reading, but she was on a mission.

Never mind about the papers, Wilder. Those papers didn't contain a canister of Super 8 film.

It seemed odd that Chuck Knapp used such a low-tech medium, when he taught such a high-tech class, but that's what he was comfortable with. If she found any Super 8 film, it wouldn't belong to Saxby. Based on the equipment in the room, he used only the latest in digital technology.

She was searching Saxby's camera bag when the phone rang. The first ring made her nearly jump out of her skin. With the second ring she realized it had to be Lark warning her of Saxby's return. She had her hand on the doorknob when the phone rang a third time.

She let out her breath in a rush. It was just a phone call. Instantly she made the decision to continue her search. After all, she'd gotten in here. There was no need to turn tail and run. No need to panic. If Dorothy got Saxby pontificating, Rachel might have hours. At any rate, she was almost done.

She searched the windowsills, discovered an address book behind the television — an odd place to keep an address book, but she replaced it — and a warm can of Dr Pepper. Stretching out on the floor, she checked under the beds, not expecting to find anything. She wished she had flipped up the dust ruffle so it wasn't quite so dark, and prayed there were no spiders. She hated spiders.

Then the door opened.

Her first thought was it had to be another door. Maybe Furtive Man stepping out.

Her second thought was she was imagining things. Lark would have called to warn her.

By the time she had her next thought, she was completely under the bed and no longer dismayed by the fact that it was dark in the room. Now she really hoped there were no spiders, although insects were the least of her worries.

Saxby's room, like hers, had two four-posters. Between them, she had somehow chosen to scoot under the bed closest to the door, which was also the one Guy Saxby — or somebody — sat on.

The springs creaked and sagged.

Rachel sucked in her stomach and breathed through her mouth.

A shoe hit the floor — another wing tip. This one appeared to be black. The other shoe dropped quickly, and the springs creaked again.

Good job, Wilder. How could this be any worse?

Above her, Saxby blew his nose rather loudly, and for long enough that she might have made her escape if only nose-blowing made a person blind and deaf.

It could have been worse if he'd come in with Dorothy. The fact she could think such a thing at a time like this made her feel like laughing. *Think, Wilder.*

Rachel sobered up and considered her options. She could come out and admit what she'd been up to. Saxby wouldn't kill her, not with Lark aware she was there, but he might turn her in. He also might want to know how she'd managed to get in his room. She would have to tell him, and then the cheerful maid would be in trouble. That would be bad.

Or, she could stay where she was and hope for a good opportunity to sneak out of the room. When she played the second option out in her head, she had been able to look at the door and choose her moment. That wasn't the reality of the situation. She could see the door, but Saxby had stretched out on the bed, turned on the TV, and was flipping through the channels — a practice that drove Rachel nuts even at the best of times. This was not the best of times.

Her mind conjured a third option. Saxby, with sharp instincts and keen senses, might have realized there was somebody in his room and was simply waiting for the right moment to pounce. Maybe he had even turned the TV on as cover.

The phone rang.

Once again Rachel jumped.

The bed creaked as, presumably, Saxby rolled over to answer. He picked the phone up midway through the second ring.

"Hello? *Hello?*" he said, and then he slammed down the receiver.

It was definitely Saxby's voice, Rachel heard, and it must have been Lark's warning call. *Nice timing, Drummond.*

Of course, she couldn't really blame Lark for her predicament. It had been her own brilliant idea, and now she was stuck under a bed in a man's room, and she might have to stay here all night. She would have to stay awake. Not that there was the remotest chance she would ever sleep, but if she did she might snore, or talk in her sleep, or do

232

something that would give her away.

Maybe *he* would snore. Then she would know it was time to bolt.

Stay calm, Wilder. By now Lark had to know Rachel was in trouble, and she would do something. Maybe set off the fire alarm? Or maybe something more subtle, like coming up and knocking on the door. Lark could say Dorothy needed him, and lure him down to the second floor.

Rachel lay under the bed for what seemed like hours. Finally, she forced herself to relax. She was glad when Saxby found a movie he wanted to watch — a remake of *Sabrina,* starring Harrison Ford. Rachel followed the script with the dialogue, pleased at least that the housekeeping staff had been diligent about sweeping under the bed. There was no dust, no cobwebs, nothing to make her feel like sneezing. Or coughing.

A giggle bubbled up in her throat.

Or crying.

All of which seemed like distinct possibilities. In fact, Rachel began to feel like she might fall asleep under there, given a long enough stay.

Guy Saxby's feet hit the floor with a soft *thump,* and he padded into the bathroom.

A shower! That's what you need. Instead she heard what sounded like a gallon of water being poured from a great height. At least he'd be facing away from the door.

She started to slide out from under the bed when she heard the shower start up. He must have picked up her urging. Drawing a deep breath, she prepared herself to make a run for it, when she heard him come out and slide open the closet door. Flattening herself out, she waited for him to return to the bathroom.

Why didn't he close the door? She would have shut the door if she were taking a shower, even in a room where nobody else was supposed to be. Then she heard his voice again.

Was he talking to himself? No, he was singing!

Rachel inched out from under the bed. She could only hope he had his face turned away from the door. He belted out a Billy Joel song, "The Longest Time," alternating between the lead singer's line and the backup, making it impossible to judge in which direction he stood.

Just go for it, Wilder.

She rolled over the wing tips by the bed, resisted the temptation to peer into the bathroom, and felt grateful this time that the light in the room was dim. Making it past the open bathroom, she yanked on the door. Saxby had been cautious, and had fastened the night latch. The door opened a half inch, and then stopped with a *clank.*

Rachel bit her lip as the singing stopped.

"Hey!" came from inside the shower. "Who's there?"

Rachel shut the door and backed into the closet, her hand touching his jacket. A small, round object the size of a can of chewing tobacco dented the inner pocket. The film!

She heard him climb out of the shower. Lifting the small tin from his pocket, she bolted for the door. Sliding the chain out of its track, she swung open the door, bolted out into the hall, and slammed the door shut behind her.

Talk about not choosing your moment!

Fortunately the hallway was empty. Racing down the stairs, she skidded around corners and didn't stop until she was in front of her own room. Banging noisily, she ran through a quick scenario of how she would be caught. Saxby would catch up to her, the maid who had let her in upstairs would choose just this moment to come down the hall, and security would storm the stairways. And then Lark yanked open the door.

Behind her, Cecilia and Dorothy sat,

open-mouthed, on the beds. "Oh my."

Rachel burst inside, and slammed the door behind her. "Bad news," she gasped. "Guy Saxby's a thief!"

It took her a few moments to catch her breath, and to listen to Lark's apology.

Dorothy and Cecilia had appeared at the door with Saxby shortly after Rachel had gone upstairs. Lark had done her best to keep him occupied, and had called as soon as he left. Unfortunately, Dorothy had wanted to know who she was calling and Lark had let the phone ring too long.

Up until then, Dorothy had sat stoically at the end of Rachel's bed. Now she wanted answers. "What were you thinking, going up to Guy's room?"

"I was thinking Knapp might have been right with his accusations." Rachel pulled the small tin from her pocket.

The others gasped. Dorothy's eyes looked shiny and wet.

"Oh my," whispered Cecilia.

Dorothy's expression hardened. "We don't know what's in there."

"We can guess," said Lark. "Open it."

Inside was a small reel with inch-wide film.

CHAPTER 15

Rachel pulled the reel out of its tin holder, and grasped the film by its edges. She held it up to the light and studied the positive image frame by frame.

There was no doubt that the film was shot in a swamp. The sun shone brightly through tall Cyprus and tupelo trees draped in Spanish moss. An old-growth forest covered the highlands, peat blanketed the ground. She could tell by the angle that Knapp and Becker were standing on low ground when the film was taken. A deer path meandered through the forest, the understory thick with a tangle of dead trees and limbs. A small rise caused the path to bend in the distance. Above the curve was a spot of red.

The next nine or ten frames told the story. A large black-and-white bird with a red crest and a white bill flew by, landing on a nearby tree. Its flight was straight, the bird looked huge, and its trailing wing feathers formed a white saddle on its back.

"The ivory-billed woodpecker," said Lark. Awe softened her voice. "You were right all along, Rae."

Dorothy looked crestfallen. "He lied."

If Dorothy's disappointment in Saxby overshadowed her enthusiasm about the bird, she had to be heartbroken. Rachel reached out and patted her arm.

"What else has he lied about?"

Cecilia moved to comfort her sister, but Dorothy pushed her away. "I'm going to bed."

Rachel wound the film back onto the reel and placed it back in the can. She jerked her head in the direction of Dorothy and Cecilia's room. "What do we do?"

"We turn the old goat in," said Cecilia. She seemed only too happy to hang Saxby out in the wind.

"How?" said Rachel. "Saxby stole the film from Knapp, but I took it from Saxby. It's his word against ours about who took it in the first place. Not only that, I broke into his room and there are witnesses." She told them about Furtive Man and the maid.

"So I guess that means we can't contact Detective Stone?" asked Lark.

Rachel nodded.

The three of them sat in silence, then Rachel had an idea. "I know. Tomorrow morning we can give the film back to Chuck Knapp."

The first test came at breakfast. Guy Saxby had followed them into the dining room, and Rachel struggled to keep a straight face when he sat down next to Dorothy and she elbowed him in the ribs.

"What a night I had," he said, rubbing his side. "Someone broke into my room. I was in the shower, so I grabbed a towel and took up the chase. It's not the first time my room has been violated."

Cecilia picked that moment to choke on her sticky bun.

"Was anything missing?" asked Rachel, curious about his response.

His jaw tightened, but he shook his head. "Not that I could tell. And I didn't catch the bastard. I ended up locking myself out of my room, in the hallway, dripping wet, wearing only a towel." He seemed perplexed when Dorothy didn't react.

"What did you do?" asked Lark.

"I called security from the phone on the hall table, and then one of the housekeeping staff came along. She took pity on me, and said my wife and I should be more careful. I have no idea what she was talking about."

This time it was Rachel's turn to choke.

Right then Evan Kearns appeared in the restaurant. "There you are. Guy, I need to speak with you."

Saxby wiped his mouth. "Sure, Evan. Is something wrong?"

"Outside."

Rachel and Lark exchanged glances.

Saxby set down his napkin and stood. "I'll be right back, ladies."

"Maybe not," Kearns said, steering him away.

Rachel watched the two of them talk in the foyer. By the gestures, it appeared something serious had happened.

Saxby returned to the table, but his demeanor had changed. He sat down, stared at the remains of his breakfast, and shook his head as if to clear it.

"What's happened?" asked Rachel, sensing he needed some prompting.

"Chuck Knapp is dead."

Her skin tingled. The rest of the women looked like they'd gone into shock.

"What do you mean, dead?" asked Rachel.

"Dead, as in murdered," said Saxby. "Shot. Sometime last night. Kearns is shutting down the convention."

"Oh my," said Cecilia.

Dorothy's skin turned ashen, and Lark's mouth dropped open. Rachel fingered the film can in her pocket.

"That's terrible," said Lark.

"What time was he killed?" asked Rachel. Her mind was doing the math.

"What kind of question is that?" asked Saxby. "How should I know?"

"Kearns didn't say?" If it happened early enough, Saxby was in the clear. He might be a thief, but he wasn't a murderer.

Dorothy seemed to follow her train of thought. "It's important you try and remember, Guy."

Saxby rubbed his forehead. "He said the police knocked on his door around ten. We were still having fun in the bar about then."

Who else had been in the bar? Rachel wracked her brain trying to remember. Patricia Anderson had been helping the waitress, who had been caught unprepared by the number of birders descending upon the bar that late.

Their suspect list was dwindling. With Knapp and Becker both dead it was safe to assume the murders were connected, which cleared Sonja. What possible reason would she have to kill Knapp? If Saxby was right about the time of Knapp's death, he was off the hook, too. He was in the bar, and then in his room at the time Knapp was killed. Rachel could attest to that. Patricia Anderson was waiting tables and doing dishes. Liam Kelly had an alibi for Becker's murder, which left Wolcott, Nevin Anderson, and the Carters on the list.

"What happens now?" asked Cecilia.

"I need to make arrangements to get onto Swamper's Island," said Saxby, pushing back his chair. "I'll call you later, Dorothy."

Dorothy glanced up, her face impassive. "I don't think we have much to talk about, Guy."

He looked startled. "Did I . . . is there something wrong?"

"You might say I've had a change of heart."

Rachel, Lark, and Cecilia spent the rest of the morning trying to console Dorothy. It was tough learning someone you cared for had betrayed you. Rachel's thoughts moved to Roger. She understood firsthand how that felt.

"He's not worth it, Dot," said Cecilia.

"How could I have been so stupid?" Dorothy seemed angrier with herself than with Guy.

"You were duped," said Cecilia. "It happens."

Dorothy looked like Cecilia had slapped her. "It never happens to me."

By afternoon she had stopped feeling sorry for herself, and self-pity had turned to anger.

"How do we know that Knapp was killed when Guy said he was?" she demanded. "He probably lied about that, too."

A valid point, thought Rachel. It was time to see Detective Stone and hand over the film.

The Brunswick Police Department was located on Mansfield Street in a two-story brick building with white trim. Large mullioned windows faced the street, and a black awning shaded the front steps. Rachel parked the rental car in a one-hour spot, and she and Lark jaywalked to the entrance. Dorothy was gunning for Saxby, so she and Cecilia had stayed behind.

Inside the building, marble-tiled floors shone with fresh polish. Institutional-green paint covered the walls. Large framed photographs of the Brunswick Police Department chiefs from 1927 onward hung on the walls.

A doorway on the left stood open, and a

young officer in blue looked up as Rachel and Lark entered.

"May I help you?"

"We're looking for Detective Stone," said Rachel.

"May I tell him who's calling?"

"Rachel Wilder and Lark Drummand."

The officer in blue picked up the phone receiver and dialed a number.

Detective Stone didn't keep them waiting. He came in through the open door, and ushered them across the hall into his office. Pointing to two wooden chairs with green leather seat cushions, he moved behind a large wooden desk and clasped his hands on its polished surface. "What can I do for you?"

"We found this." Rachel pushed the four-inch flat film canister across the desktop towards him. "It's Knapp's movie."

He looked confused. "That's the one he claimed was missing last night?"

Was it just last night? Rachel nodded

"And you found it?" He seemed skeptical.

"Yes." Rachel lifted her chin. It wasn't exactly a lie. She had discovered it when she wasn't searching. Still, she couldn't meet his gaze.

"Care to tell me where?"

Now came the tricky part. "It was in Guy

Saxby's possession."

"Does he know you have it?"

"We hope not," said Lark.

Rachel started to explain, but Detective Stone waved his hand in the air. "I don't want to know. Anything you say may incriminate you, and it doesn't matter anyway, since I can't prove it was ever in his possession." He glared at them through small dark eyes. "Did it ever occur to you, when you were stealing this treasure," he held up the tape, "that you were interfering in a police investigation?"

"Yes," admitted Rachel and Lark in unison.

Detective Stone sighed. "But that didn't matter."

It was more of a statement than a question, but they both replied. "No."

Rachel shrugged. "You couldn't look for it. We could. Now that we know he stole the film, the question we all want answered is, Did Saxby kill Becker and Knapp?"

"Why kill Knapp if he already had the film?" asked Stone.

"Maybe to shut Knapp up about who he thought had stolen it," said Lark.

Detective Stone shook his head. "You women are a piece of work." He rubbed his short curly hair, and flashed them a bright smile.

Rachel leaned forward. "Can you tell us what time Knapp was murdered?" It was a reasonable question, and he had no reason to hide the answer.

"The coroner estimates between nine-thirty and eleven."

"Then he's in the clear," said Lark. "Are you satisfied now, Rae?"

"How do you now Saxby's in the clear?" asked Detective Stone.

At that point, Rachel confessed. She told him everything about her adventure the night before. Detective Stone didn't even try not to laugh.

Once he'd gotten control of himself, he said, "I'm ready to hear your theories now. Who remains on your suspect list?"

Rachel held up a finger. "Victor Wolcott."

"The head of the Hyde Island Authority?" Detective Stone jotted his name on a pad of paper. "What makes you suspect him?"

Lark filled him in on Wolcott's development plans.

"He and Nevin Anderson might even be working together," added Rachel. She explained how the discovery of a rare species on the swampland might have derailed the sale.

"But it helps with the trade," Detective Stone pointed out.

"Maybe not," said Rachel. "If the state doesn't have to sacrifice the eighty acres because the swampland is protected under federal law, the state comes out ahead. They keep their land, their money, and the swampland remains undeveloped."

He scratched his head again. "Anderson and Wolcott are hunting buddies. Both of them know their way around a weapon, and either one of them could have taken pot-shots at you from the golf course."

"Then there's the Carter brothers and Fancy." Rachel told him about seeing Dwight with a rifle the day of the Swamper's Island fiasco.

"Why would he care what happens?"

"Fancy stands to make a lot of money if the land trade or a development happens. She makes nothing if both deals fall through. Her sons might be protecting their interest."

"I've talked to those boys," said Detective Stone. "And their mother. She wants to sell the land. Those boys would be happier with the status quo."

Well, that ruled out the Carter boys as suspects. As for Fancy, Rachel couldn't imagine her using more than her wiles to try and finagle a deal. That left Anderson and Wolcott. Were they in this together, or was each man out for himself?

"You're going to stay out of this," said Detective Stone as if reading her mind. "Thanks for bringing this in." He picked up the film can, and then shook it. Popping it open, he showed them it was empty.

Rachel's stomach tightened, and her skin tingled. "It was there last night. I put it in the nightstand." She looked at Lark.

"I didn't take it."

"How about your friends?" asked Detective Stone.

"No," said Rachel. "They'd have no reason to take it." Then a sickening thought crept into her mind. "When we came back up from breakfast our room was made up."

"Why would the maid steal the film?" asked Detective Stone.

"She wouldn't," said Rachel. "But Nevin Anderson would. Maybe one of the Andersons took it, and made up the room to make us think the maid had been there. We were in the restaurant for at least an hour."

"Okay," he said, closing the canister and setting it aside on his desk. "I'll check into it. Now, you two, go back to the hotel, pack your bags, and go home. No more digging around. No more hiding under beds. You leave tomorrow, right?"

"Monday," said Lark.

"Then go bird-watching. That's what you came for."

They followed his advice. Back at the hotel Dorothy was still in a funk, so Rachel took matters into her own hands. They all wanted a chance to see the bird of a lifetime, and even if the festival was canceled, the Carters were offering the Okefenokee Swamp Tour. Rachel secured the last four spots on the bus. The next morning, she climbed out of bed before the alarm went off.

"Rise and shine," said Rachel. "It's six a.m."

Lark rolled over and stretched. "Oh boy, another bus ride."

"Yes, but this time we'll actually get to see something," said Rachel. She knocked on the door connecting their suite to Dorothy and Cecilia's. "Rise and shine."

"Watch out," Lark yelled, "it's Tour Guide Barbie. I think the Lucy Bell gals have gotten Rachel in their clutches."

"Oh my," said Cecilia. "Are we having fun yet?"

"We'd better be," said Rachel. "It's our last day."

By six-thirty, Dorothy was the one all put

together. After adding finishing touches to her hair, she started packing her backpack. "Okay, ladies, we need sunscreen, water, field books, cameras, sunglasses, binoculars . . ."

"Don't forget bug spray," said Cecilia.

"Can you believe it? We're going out to see a bird thought to be extinct," said Dorothy. "I may not be having a Big Year, but if we spot the ivory-billed, it will be one of the best."

"There are no guarantees, Dot."

"No, but I have a feeling."

Rachel was pleased to see Dorothy in such a good mood, and her enthusiasm was contagious. Everyone on the bus seemed to catch her spirit. Everyone's hopes for seeing some unusual species were high.

The bus ride was uneventful. Lark dozed. Cecilia and Dorothy compared field notes from the week. Rachel enjoyed the view from the windows. The marshes dissipated, and tall pine forests lined the roads.

She sat up straighter when they passed the turnoff where they had idled on Friday. The spear of land called Swamper's Island tapered off to the west, cut off from the mainland by a large swath of brackish water. A small wooden bridge behind a wire fence bridged the gap — one side supported by

Swamper's Island, the other supported by Carter land.

The turn-in for the Okefenokee Swamp Tours camp was a half mile farther down the road. A small trailer sported a large sign declaring it the Okefenokee Swamp Tours Convenience Store. The cutout of a large alligator waving a safari hat stood on its hind legs supporting the sign. Several outbuildings were scattered about, and several motorboats were tied up to the docks. In the distance, she could see the National Wildlife Refuge building.

"Look who drove themselves rather than travel with the hoi polloi," said Cecilia as the bus jolted to a stop.

Rachel glanced out the window. Nevin Anderson and Victor Wolcott were unloading gear from the back of a beige sedan.

As their group moved en masse toward the small convenience store, Wolcott and Anderson headed for the canoes. Rachel watched them negotiate with Fancy, before loading their gear into a dark green canoe.

Were they going out on the field trip, or did they plan to venture into the swamp alone?

The last case that Anderson stowed looked long and padded. A rifle case?

Rachel's heart beat faster. "Did you see

that?" she asked Lark.

"See what?"

"Nevin Anderson just loaded a gun into that canoe."

CHAPTER 16

"A gun?" echoed Lark. "Maybe it was fishing gear."

"In a gun case?"

"Let's go, ladies," interrupted Kearns, shepherding them toward the convenience store. "We haven't got time for you to stand around and yak. Make sure you have everything you need before heading to the boats — bottled water, snacks, and wet bags."

Lark, Cecilia, and Dorothy did his bidding. Rachel hung back and watched Anderson and Wolcott push off from shore. Wolcott sat in the middle, hunched over, his portly physique covered in khaki. A fishing hat covered his head, shielding his nose from the hot sun. Anderson, on the other hand, looked like he was headed off for a round of golf. He wore a collared short-sleeved shirt and shorts. A Hyde Island Club Hotel visor shaded the angles of his face.

Steering them into open water, Anderson looked up, smiled, and waved.

Rachel scampered to catch up to the others. Perhaps they'd see them out on the water. She was curious to know where they were headed.

The four of them bought four waters, a box of granola bars, and what amounted to four giant Ziploc baggies. Rachel bought a map. After stuffing their belongings into the bags, they stopped and used the bathrooms, and then headed for the canoes. By the time they arrived at the boats, Wolcott and Anderson were out of sight.

"Is hunting allowed in the swamp?" she asked Dwayne while he and Dwight measured their party for oar lengths and handed out orange life preservers.

Dwayne's head snapped up. "No. Why?"

"Ah, I . . ." She wrestled with her answer, and then chose the truth. "I just thought I saw someone loading a gun into one of the canoes."

Dwight and Dwayne exchanged glances. Dwayne made a slight gesture with his head, and Dwight took off toward the store.

"Thanks for the heads-up," said Dwayne, bending back over the life preserver ties. "Hunting is restricted to private property and special shoots. The deer population can get out of hand. But we're not in deer season. And this ain't private property." He smiled his dazzling smile, and gestured toward a canoe. "Now, let's get you seated."

Dorothy and Cecilia were assigned to one canoe, Lark and Rachel to another. The rest broke into pairs.

"This is how it works," said Dwayne, with a wink at Rachel.

Either he had an eye condition, or he was a flirt. She made a mental note to tell him about Kirk.

"Stay seated in the canoes. The person in front steers, the person in back paddles. Together you'll find your rhythm. You first." Dwayne pointed at Lark and Rachel.

"You steer," said Lark.

Rachel stepped forward.

Dwayne grabbed hold of her elbow, and helped her into the canoe. "The long narrow construction makes the canoe a little tippy. The person steering sits near the front." Once Rachel was settled he pointed at Lark. "The paddler is going to push off, and jump in. You need to get your fanny on that seat there." He pointed to the seat behind Rachel. "Put your oar in the boat, and steady yourself by keeping two hands on either side."

Lark shoved off and missed getting in the

canoe. Rachel floated out a ways and struggled to paddle back on her own. On the second try, they both managed to get into the boat, but the canoe tipped side to side and threatened to take on water.

"Sit down," ordered Dwayne.

Lark sat. It took a moment for the boat to steady itself, and then they were floating free. The canoe drifted, and bumped into one of the powerboats tied up at the docks.

"Push off," said Dwayne. "Now turn around slowly. That's right."

Rachel and Lark found their rhythm quickly. Paddling and steering was easier than mounting and dismounting. The biggest challenge was not running into another member of their small flotilla. Cecilia and Dorothy hit the water like old pros.

There were sixteen canoes in all, plus one for each of the Carters joining the group on the water. Dwight Carter had never come back. Dwayne took up the middle and Fancy Carter — in skintight khakis, a white tank top, and a safari hat — acted as their tour guide.

"Indian tribes used to live in the swamp," she explained. "The last being the Seminoles, who were driven into Florida around 1850. In 1891, the land was purchased by the Suwannee Canal Company. Their intent was to drain the land for logging and to grow crops. Their leader, Captain Henry Jackson, and his crew spent three years digging the Suwannee Canal. When economic recession led the company to bankruptcy, the land was sold to the Hebard Cypress Company, and a railroad was built into the west edge of the swamp. In just under thirty years, over four hundred thirty-one million board feet of Cypress was removed from the Okefenokee.

"Nowadays, we work to preserve the natural wonders of the swamp. Research has been done on everything from bacteria to black bears. Prescribed burns help maintain a natural vegetation process, and trees are being replanted."

"What about endangered species?" asked a woman sharing a canoe with her young daughter.

Dwayne looked perturbed.

"Special emphasis is placed on the two *known* species in the swamp," said Fancy. "The red-cockaded woodpeckers and the indigo snakes."

"Snakes?" said Lark.

"Indigos are large blue-black snakes that grow up to nine feet long," said Dwayne. "They're not dangerous. It's the other snakes you need to watch out for." He seemed to take pleasure in Lark's obvious distress. Rachel felt a little squeamish herself.

"What kind of other snakes?" asked Lark.

"Coral snakes, copperheads, rattlers. Cottonmouths are the ones you're most likely to see from the water. Some grow to be eight feet long. In fact, we should have warned you to stay away from the banks. The snakes like to climb into the trees, and they have been known to drop into the boats at times."

Lark looked pale.

"That happened once, Dwayne," said Fancy. "He's just trying to scare you. Though, if it happens, abandon your canoe. Cottonmouths don't like people, but they get aggressive if they feel trapped."

"Of course, in the water, the alligators can be a problem," said Dwayne. "Especially in the spring." He pointed at a five-foot alligator on the bank of the canal. The gator opened its jaws and hissed. "They have young 'uns to protect this time of year. If you stay in the canoes and away from the mounds, you'll be fine."

Rachel pointed to a tree and pretended to read, PLEASE DO NOT SWIM.

Lark took her paddle and sent a shower of brackish water into the canoe.

"Hey."

Dorothy shot them both a stern look. "How large is the refuge?"

"At present?" Fancy swiveled around in her seat. "Three hundred ninety-six thousand acres, 90 percent of which are protected federal lands. The Okefenokee is one the most well-preserved freshwater areas in America."

She sounded proud of that, thought Rachel.

"The Indians used to call this place the 'land of the trembling earth.' Peat deposits up to fifteen feet thick cover much of the swamp floor, and these deposits are so unstable in areas that if you stomp on the earth, you can cause the trees and bushes to tremble. The waters are slow-moving and tea colored from the tannic acid released from decaying plants. You can swim in it, and you can drink it, though we don't recommend it. It's about as acidic as a cola drink."

They paddled about three miles out, moving from the main canal onto the Chesser Prairie, an open-water area with white and yellow water lilies, blue iris, and miles of floating chunks of peat.

"These floating islands are called 'batteries,' " explained Fancy. "They start as peat 'blowups,' small clumps of peat dislodged by the alligators and snapping turtles, and they provide a surface for seeds to germinate. Fast-growing herbs and grasses such as spike rush, beak rush, wiry bladderwort, sundews, and others move in, forming a firm surface that can support larger herbs and grasses such as chain fern, bur-marigold, yellow-eyed grass, redroot, maiden cane, and others."

Rachel didn't recognize the names of any of the ferns and grasses, but they sounded exotic.

"Eventually, some of the batteries grow firm enough to support shrubs like bay and blackgum trees. When a battery becomes rooted to the bottom of the swamp they're called 'houses.' Cypress trees will eventually grow on houses, and that changes the face of the swamp."

Dwayne stood up in his canoe and pushed on the side of a peat battery. The edge bobbed into the water. "Alligators sometimes wait for an animal, like a wild pig, to fall into the water and get trapped under the lip of one of these batteries, and then they feed on it."

"It would make a great place to dump a body," said Cecilia.

With that image in mind, the group

pushed deeper onto the prairie. Far in the distance, Rachel caught sight of Wolcott and Anderson paddling in a northwesterly direction.

They must be headed for Swamper's Island, she thought, which made sense. The Carters had barred them access across their land.

She watched the men paddling as Fancy explained how fire was important to the swamp — the cypress were fire-resistant, but the understory burned — creating the old cypress forests. By the time she had moved onto talking about old-growth cypress forests, Wolcott and Anderson were out of sight.

Rachel turned around to look at Lark. She seemed to have noticed them, too.

The men had made much better time than the group, which had stopped to birdwatch along the way. Prothonotary warblers, commonly known as the swamp canary, had flitted in the cypress knees along the canal. Bright yellow with blue wings, its *sweet, sweet, sweet* call had announced its presence at every turn. Yellow-rumped warblers, commonly known as butter-butts, Northern parula, and Carolina wrens had joined in to entertain them as well.

Now, sandhill cranes demanded their attention. The large, graceful birds trumpeted their movements. Osprey flew overhead. Anihingas, cormorants, herons, and egrets adorned the lush green grasses of the swamp.

"Can you walk on the batteries?" asked the young girl with her mother.

"It's not advised," said Fancy, "The tangle of roots creates a porous surface, sort of like a scouring pad. It will hold you, but only if you keep moving. The trees swing and sway." She tipped her canoe side to side, and the young girl's eyes widened. "Remember, that's why it's called the 'trembling earth.' "

Before long, talk turned to issues of conservation, then Dorothy said, "Tell us some more swamp legends."

This time Fancy deferred to Dwayne.

"Okay. There used to be a form of communication between swamp dwellers known as 'hollerin'.' It's a form of yodeling that traveled for miles." Dwayne spread his arms wide. "When someone got lost in the swamp, hollerin' helped others figure out their position. During the bootlegging years . . ." He looked at the young girl. "You know what those are, don't you?"

She scrunched up her face, and shook her head.

"Those were the years when drinkin' was outlawed by the government, and people made illegal whiskey to sell."

The girl looked to her mother for confirmation. Her mother nodded.

"Anyway, there was this one bootlegger who had a big still set up on Bugscratch Island. It was a great island for bootlegging because it sits right off the Suwannee Canal." He went on to describe the island, and the still, and a craggy old man named Henry MacNair. "According to legend, old Henry made a lot of money selling his whiskey, and he buried it all on Bugscratch Island."

"Is it still there?" asked Dorothy.

"You're jumping ahead of the story." He waited a beat, and then continued. "One night, the police came out to arrest him. But old Henry, he was smart. He set up an ambush. A shoot-out ensued, and when the powder settled old Henry was nowhere to be found. Neither was his money. The police dug so many holes in Bugscratch Island that it sank to the bottom of the swamp. People claim that the ghost of old Henry MacNair still travels these waters, and that if you listen real close sometimes you can still hear him hollerin'. Some folks say he's trying to tell people where the treasure is buried.

Others think he's trying to lead folks deep into the swamp where they'll never be heard from again."

The silence of the group was punctuated by the noise of the swamp. Birds called in the background, an alligator bellowed, and flies buzzed.

"Have you heard him?" asked the young girl.

"You bet," said Dwayne.

A murmur ran through the boaters, then he looked at his watch.

"That does it for us," he said, paddling his canoe in a circle. "Our arrangement with the festival is that you can keep the canoes until five p.m. That's closing time, and we don't want any of you out here after dark. It's eleven o'clock now. We've taken our time getting out here, but plan on it taking you at least an hour to get back from this point. You're free to wander. Keep in hollerin' distance of each other. Anyone who wants to head back now can come with us."

Fancy and Dwayne headed back with three of the canoes in their wake. Most of the others headed off toward the south, in the direction of the sandhill cranes. Rachel turned north.

"Where are you going?" called Cecilia. "Everyone else is going —"

"Shhhhh." Rachel exaggerated her whisper. "I know where they're going." Rachel told them what she had witnessed, the loading of what looked like a gun case into the canoe, and their disappearance to the north.

"I saw them, too," confirmed Lark.

"They were headed northeast," said Rachel.

"Are you sure that's north?" asked Cecilia. "It think that's west."

Dorothy adjusted her sun visor. "The sun rises in the east and sets in the west. Trust me, Cec, Rae's right. That's north."

"What do you think they were doing with a gun?" asked Cecilia.

Dorothy looked at her sister askance. "Hiding the weapon that killed Becker and Knapp."

Rachel shook her head. "Why bring it this far into the swamp, or risk someone seeing them with it? No, I think they're hunting."

Cecilia turned around and stared at Rachel. "Hunting for what?"

"What do they both want dead?"

The others stared at Rachel, and then one by one understanding bloomed on their faces.

"Oh my."

Rachel nodded. "I think they're planning on shooting the ivory-billed woodpecker.

With both Becker and Knapp dead and the film destroyed, if the bird was gone, life reverts back to normal. The land trade will go through. Everyone gets their money." Rachel remembered the two of them talking with Fancy and wondered if she was in on it.

"But everyone heard them talking about the bird," said Dorothy. "Someone would check it out."

"Maybe. But if no one finds anything . . ." Rachel paused to let her words sink in. "The deal might be delayed, but it wouldn't be dead."

With that, Lark started paddling faster. Rachel worked to keep the canoe headed in the right direction, and Dorothy and Cecilia fell in behind, working hard to keep pace. After better than an hour of steady paddling, Dorothy yelled, "Can we stop and rest for a minute?"

Rachel gladly shipped her oar. She wanted a chance to look at the map of the swamp she had bought.

The laminated map opened up to about the size of an eight-by-eleven sheet of paper. Judging from where they started and where they were now, she placed them halfway between the Mizell Prairie and the Christie Prairie.

Lark leaned to look over her shoulder. "How much farther do we have to go?"

"We should be able to turn east somewhere in here." Rachel pointed to the map, and held her hand up to shield her face from the sun, looking for an opening along the edge at the prairie. "Swamper's Island isn't on this map."

"What?" exclaimed Dorothy. "You mean to tell me we have been pushing through the floating peat and lilies, and we don't even know where we're headed?" She took a swig off her water bottle. "It's already getting close to twelve-thirty."

Based on Dwayne's instructions that meant, at a stiff clip, they were two hours from camp. That gave them two and a half hours to play with.

"We need to head east." Rachel pointed to the map. "I say we paddle another hour. Then, if we don't find any sign of them, we turn back."

"What are we going to do if we find them?" asked Lark.

That part of her plan was hazy. "Stop them from shooting the bird."

"How?" asked Lark, pulling her braids through a hole in the back of her cap and wiggling her fanny on the wide seat. The canoe rocked gently side to side. "By letting them shoot us?"

"Let's find them first," said Dorothy, sounding more like her old self than Rachel had heard her all week. "Then we'll think of something. Right, Rae?"

Rachel smiled, hoping she exuded more confidence than she felt. "Right."

"Oh my, here we go again," said Cecilia.

They paddled a short distance farther, and then Lark discovered a path to the east. The peat bogs closed in tighter, and Rachel had a more difficult time shoving the clumps out of the way.

"We're never going to get turned around in here," said Lark.

"Stop worrying." Rachel wasn't about to admit she was thinking the same thing. "Keep paddling."

A few more strokes brought them into more open water, and the landscape in front of them changed from floating peat to actual land. Tall cypress trees anchored the banks, with blackgum filling the understory.

"Look." Rachel pointed with her oar to a green canoe tied up a short way upstream.

"Let's go ashore here," suggested Dorothy.

A brief discussion ensued about whether it was better to tie off upstream or downstream of the men's canoe.

"Let's tie off here," said Lark, paddling toward shore. "We don't plan on them getting ahead of us."

"That's right," said Dorothy. "Grab the knee. We can pull the boats up on the backside."

Rachel crawled up into the bow, and stretched outward. Her hand brushed the bark of the cypress, and then something moved on the ground.

CHAPTER 17

Rachel froze. An eight-foot-long alligator opened its mouth, hissed, and lunged. Rachel yanked back her hand and screamed.

At least, she thought she had screamed. Her mouth came open, but all she heard was the blood rushing in her ears.

Throwing herself back into the canoe, she clamped one hand over her mouth and with the other frantically signaled for Lark to back paddle.

"It won't follow," said Dorothy, her voice low and calm. "It's protecting its nest."

Rachel's heart banged against her rib cage, threatening to burst through her chest. Her breath came in sharp, short bursts.

"Breathe, Rae. Deep breaths. See, it's okay." Dorothy pointed to the alligator backing up onto the land. Cecilia and Lark both looked as white as the water lily flowers, a stark contrast to the lush greens of the swamp and a dead giveaway of how scared they were.

"Why don't we pull up there?" suggested Cecilia, pointing to a spot nearer to Anderson and Wolcott's canoe.

"Because we don't want them to know we're here," said Dorothy.

Rachel remained speechless. Inhale two . . . three . . . four, hold two . . . three . . . four, exhale two . . . three . . . four. It was an exercise she had learned in yoga class to calm herself down.

Cecilia looked confused. "Aren't we planning to tell them?"

Finally, Rachel's heart rate slowed enough that she drew a final deep breath and exhaled loudly and long. "She's right, Dorothy. We have to let them know we're here. How else are we going to stop them?"

Besides, after her encounter with the alligator, it made sense to her that they should start making more noise. Hadn't Dwayne said the swamp creatures steered clear if they knew you were coming? The last thing she wanted was to surprise another creature like the last one.

"Not only that," said Lark. "If Anderson and Wolcott hear us, they might just hightail it back to their boat."

"Or start gunning for us," said Dorothy.

That thought gave Rachel pause. She

pictured the men stuffing their bodies under the batteries in the swamp. The darn alligator would dine out all spring. Maybe it was better to keep their mouths shut.

She went with the compromise. "I say we keep quiet until we know where they are. Meanwhile, let's pull the canoes up upstream from where their canoe is. There isn't apt to be an alligator too near where the men went ashore, and we can hide the canoes from sight behind that large cypress knee."

Stuffing down her fear, Rachel scrambled out first, then held the canoes steady while the rest of them clambered ashore. The ground felt spongy, but solid. Cecilia slipped, knocking a chunk of peat free with her foot.

Dorothy batted it away. "Watch it."

While Dorothy tied up the boats, using a talent she had mastered years ago teaching Girl Scouts how to tie knots for a merit badge, Rachel rescued her camera cell phone out of her wet bag. It showed no signal, but she might get a signal farther inland and, if they came upon Wolcott and Anderson doing anything illegal, the phone just might come in handy.

"All set?" asked Dorothy, brushing her hands together when she tied the last knot.

"Ready," said Lark. She didn't look anxious to go first, so Rachel took up the lead.

"Follow me."

A narrow deer path ran back through the woods. From the way the leaves were disturbed, she suspected Anderson and Wolcott had followed it, too.

"Watch where you step," warned Dorothy. "Some snakes, like the pygmy rattler, like to hide in the leaf litter."

Great, just great.

How many types of snakes had Dwayne said lived in the swamp? Thirty-four? Of course not all of those had been poisonous, but at least a third of them were.

They were a hundred yards in when a flash of red, black, and yellow an the deer path caught Rachel's attention. She stopped dead in her tracks. Lark walked right into her, followed by Dorothy and Cecilia. A four-person pile up.

"What's wrong?" asked Lark.

Rachel pointed to the ground about ten feet ahead. "Do you see that?"

A small snake with red, yellow, and black bands slithered into the brush.

" 'Red on yellow will kill a fellow,' " recited Dorothy. "I think it's poisonous."

"Are you sure it's not 'black on yellow, deadly fellow'?" asked Cecilia.

"Yes, I'm sure, Cec. I taught science class for twenty years." Dorothy turned back to Rachel. "Either way, don't touch it."

Like she needed some sort of sign, or even a person, to tell her that. "Don't worry."

Rachel counted to twenty, giving the snake ample time to go on its way, and then pressed on. A glance at her watch caused her to quicken her step. They'd used up another hour, and their time was dwindling.

After about a mile, she stopped. The island had grown sandier as they walked and the tree canopy more open. Standing near the bottom of a small dip, she peered through the trees. Ahead the path turned just before a small rise.

Her adrenaline surged.

"This is it," she said softly. "This is the place in the film." She pointed the landmarks out to the others. "I remember the lush hillside, and the bend in the path."

A male voice spoke from the other side of the rise. All four women dropped to the ground.

"Do you see anything?" he said.

Victor Wolcott? Rachel thought so by his polished manner of speech.

"No, but this looks like the place Saxby described."

There was no question that the whinier

voice belonged to Nevin Anderson.

"Guy would never have told them a thing if he knew what they were up to," whispered Dorothy.

Rachel's heart ached that Dorothy still believed in him after all they'd discovered.

"Did you hear that?" asked Anderson. Stress made his voice crack in pitch.

Had he heard Dorothy speaking?

"Hear what?"

"It sounded like a rustling in the trees over there."

Rachel could see the barrel of a gun above the green vines on the hillside. She put her finger to her lips and gestured for the others to move off the path. Then she signaled that she was going to try and go around for a better look. Lark followed her, sticking so close on her heels that Rachel periodically kicked her.

"Back off, Lark," she whispered.

"What the hell is all this crap?" Wolcott was saying.

Rachel heard his foot strike something.

"It looks like an old basket."

Anderson didn't seem too interested.

Rachel was down on her hands and knees now, peering around the edge of the rise. She could see Anderson and Wolcott standing in a well-trampled clearing. Several old baskets were strewn about, and two spades stuck out from dirt.

Her mind worked the information, and then it struck her. What they were looking at wasn't a hill. It was the reason two men were dead.

CHAPTER 18

Rachel signaled for Lark to move closer.

"Do you know what this is?" she whispered.

Lark shook her head.

"It's —"

A shot interrupted her sentence, and Rachel flattened herself to the ground, pulling Lark down with her.

Dwight Carter stepped into the clearing, brandishing a rifle like the one she had seen in the back of his truck.

"Drop your guns," he told the men.

"What the . . . ?" Wolcott had the decency to look scared.

Anderson mustered enough backbone to square his shoulders and put on a brave face. "This is my land."

"Shut up," Dwight ordered, gesturing with the rifle. "I told you to drop your guns."

Wolcott and Anderson both complied.

Lark had risen to her knees and tugged

on Rachel's shirt. "Come on," she mouthed, gesturing that they should go back.

Rachel dug her cell phone out of her pocket.

Still no signal.

Darn.

"Get down on your knees and put your hands behind your backs."

At least he wasn't planning to kill the men out right.

Dwight yanked a roll of duct tape out of his back pocket. "Wrap that around your friend's hands," he said to Anderson. "Then tear off a nice long piece for yourself. We're just gonna wait here until Dwayne comes and figures out what to do."

It made sense to Rachel that Dwayne was the thinker. He did most of the talking. Slapping away Lark's hand, she edged forward.

"Why the hell are you doing this?" Wolcott demanded. "You . . . we want the same thing. We came out here to kill that damn bird."

"We don't care about any stupid bird," said Dwight.

No, what they cared about was the treasure. Aponi Carter's treasure. If Rachel was right, this hill was Aponi Carter's burial mound.

Lark yanked Rachel's T-shirt again, this time hard enough that Rachel heard stitches rip. Lark was right. They needed help.

Rachel shimmied around in the tight space. Leaves rustled under her knees and her foot struck a small rock, sending it skittering across the ground.

"What was that?" asked Dwight. "Is there someone else here?"

He started in the women's direction. With no time to lose, Rachel rose to her feet and sprinted for the path, pushing Lark ahead of her.

Dwight crashed through the woods behind them.

"Run!" she yelled to the others, keeping her voice in a stage whisper. With any luck, maybe he would decide they were a family of feral pigs or a big black bear. "Untie the canoes!"

Dorothy and Cecilia glanced at each other, then made a beeline for the canoe. They might be in their mid-sixties, thought Rachel, but the two older women were fit. They seemed in optimal shape as they raced along. It must be all those years of hiking and bird-watching.

Lark's height worked to her advantage. Her long legs ate up the ground.

Rachel knew how to sprint.

The same couldn't be said about Dwight. Years of apparent beer-guzzling and bad eating habits had left him with a gut that hung over his belt, and he wheezed and stumbled as he ploughed through the woods after them.

Cecilia and Dorothy had only freed one canoe by the time Lark and Rachel reached the water. Cecilia scrambled to the back, Lark jumped in on the middle bench beside Dorothy, and Rachel leaped into the bow of the canoe, shoving away from the shore with her feet and clinging to the gunwale.

"Get your asses back here," yelled Dwight, leveling the gun.

A shot pierced the water near the bow of the canoe.

"Paddle," yelled Rachel.

Dorothy and Lark both worked their oars, but instead of going anywhere they turned the canoe in a circle.

Dwight fired another shot. This time the bullet sliced the water and made a whistling noise before plunking into canoe.

That was too close. It occurred to Rachel that Dwight might actually be shooting at the boat instead of them. Situating herself in the bow, she stuck her paddle over the side and steered them toward open water.

"Paddle together," she hollered. "Stroke.

Stroke. Stroke."

A moving target was harder to hit than a still one, and once Dorothy, Rachel, and Lark found their rhythm, the canoe started pulling away. They zigzagged toward the opposite shore with Cecilia acting as rudder. Several more shots rang out, but none of them hit their target.

Dwight leaped along the bank. Until he stumbled over the alligator.

The gator hissed and snapped.

Dwight turned and ran.

"Okay, okay," said Rachel, feeling winded more from the adrenaline coursing through her than the exertion. "He's either going to get in one of those canoes, or he's going to get in touch with Dwayne and send him to find us."

"So we need to get out of sight," said Lark.

"Why would that Carter boy shoot at us?" asked Cecilia. "I thought we had ruled them out as suspects."

"We were wrong," said Rachel. "He and his brother killed Becker and Knapp." She told them what she and Lark had seen. "It wasn't just a small rise, it was a burial mound. Knapp and Becker had it on tape. Anyone following their directions would not only find the ivory-billed woodpecker, but Aponi Carter's treasure. The Carters didn't mind the trade. What they were afraid of was being barred from the island because of the ivory-billed woodpecker."

"Do you think Fancy knows?"

Rachel shrugged. "But I'll bet she would protect her boys."

"I wonder how they knew we had the film," said Lark.

Rachel had struggled with that herself. "Maybe they didn't," she said. "Maybe stealing the film from us was Anderson's doing. Everybody knew that according to Knapp Saxby had the film, but Anderson knew something else. He knew someone had broken into Saxby's room. Remember Guy said he had notified hotel security."

Still, thought Rachel, something still didn't add up. Who had shoved the warning under their door? Patricia? She had told Katie her dad was in Brunswick. Patricia must have spotted her in the kitchen.

Shaking off the memory, Rachel forced herself to focus on the present. "The point is we're in danger out here. We have to get back to the tour office before Dwight gets word to Dwayne. In order to do that we'll need to take a different route back."

Rachel's map was in the other canoe, so she attempted reconstructing it in her mind. They had crossed the Suwannee Canal to get onto the Mizel and Christie prairies. Dwayne would expect them to back track their route and return through the Chesser Prairie. Instead, if they cut down the Suwannee Canal, they might come upon the gap of water between Swamper's Island and the Okefenokee Swamp Tour base. The inlet Rachel had noticed from the bus on the trip down. Either way, it should get them back faster, and with less chance of running into Dwayne Carter alone.

"Ah, we have another problem, Rae," said Lark.

From the fear in her friend's voice, half expected to see Dwight racing after them in the other canoe.

"What?" she asked, when the waterway appeared clear.

"We're taking on water."

Rachel had her feet pressed to the curve of the canoe. Now, looking down, she noticed the water filling the bottom of the canoe. Rachel stuck her hand down through the dark liquid, and ran her fingers low along the side of the canoe. Sure enough, a bullet had pierced the shell just in front of the middle seat. A second hole in the bottom of the canoe marked the bullet's exit.

"Dwight Carter hit his target." Rachel covered the holes with her fingers. "Cecilia, we need something to use as plugs. A handkerchief, a bandana, anything I can wad up and stick in here that will slow down the water."

Dorothy set down her paddle.

"No, you guys keep paddling."

Rachel settled for the wet bag. Biting the corner off of one end, she ripped the bag up the center. Twisting the bottom into a cone, she tried stuffing it down into the hole.

"It's working."

Or it was until she tried plugging the hole on the bottom of the canoe.

A loud crack filled the air.

"What was that?" Lark swiveled her head and looked around.

It had sounded like a shot.

"Damn," said Rachel, her fingers worrying the holes. She found a large rent in the bottom of the canoe.

"What?" Lark demanded.

"It split."

Lark bent forward. "What split?"

"The canoe. A crack just opened up in the bottom. We're taking on more water."

"Are we sinking?" asked Cecilia.

"We can't sink," insisted Lark. "Not here." Hysteria edged her voice, matching Rachel's feelings inside. Even knowing they could swim in the canal didn't quell the panic filling up her veins.

The sun was sinking in the west. In another hour they would be late getting back. In another two or three hours it would be dark.

"Let's try and stay calm," Rachel said. "The others will be missing us soon, and they'll send out a search party."

"Who?" said Lark. "Dwayne? Or Fancy?"

Lark was right.

"Paddle toward that battery over there." Rachel pointed to the east. "It has lots of trees, so it should keep us afloat."

"We can't just sit out here waiting for someone to find us," said Cecilia. "We'll be eaten by an alligator, if the biting flies don't finish us off." She slapped at a buzzing insect, and reached for the bug spray.

"Do you know the strength of an alligator's jaw is three thousand five hundred pounds per square inch?" asked Dorothy.

"Thank you for sharing," said Lark. "I could have lived without knowing that piece of information."

"But," Dorothy continued, "the muscles that open an alligator's mouth are relatively weak, so an average person — even you, Cecilia — can hold an alligator's mouth closed simply by grabbing their snout."

They reached the battery before Dorothy

could continue her science lesson, and Rachel grabbed onto a shrub. Keeping one foot anchored in the canoe, she placed one foot lightly on the battery. The water was up to her calf in the canoe, and there wasn't much time to get everyone ashore. "Dwayne did tell us we could walk on these."

"Provided we keep moving, dear," said Dorothy.

"Okay, then Lark, you go first."

"Me? Let Dorothy go first. She's the science nut."

"Fine. I'll go first." Dorothy pushed forward. Using Rachel's shoulders, she stepped onto the battery, and Rachel's foot on land submerged up to her ankle.

"Keeping moving," said Rachel. "Lark, you go behind her."

Lark caused the battery to sink even more.

"Head toward the trees," said Rachel, but Dorothy was already headed that way.

Cecilia rummaged around in the wet bag, and came up with two pairs of binoculars draped around her neck. "These are worth too much to let them go down with the ship."

"Whatever," said Rachel. "You need to go."

Cecilia headed off, her arms outstretched like a tightrope walker. Rachel took a last look at the canoe, then she pulled her foot free and immediately sank into the bog.

Walking on the "trembling earth" was like walking inside a blowup ride at a carnival, except it was wet. The ground sank and shook with every step. The trees and vegetation swayed. And if she paused, even briefly, she started to sink. At least there was no time to worry about what creatures they might encounter.

"Stay as close to the trees as possible," Dorothy shouted. "That's where the battery is the firmest. We'll head toward the cypress dome."

Rachel was happy to let Dorothy take charge. According to Dwayne, the oldest and tallest cypress trees grew near the middle of the batteries, where they eventually formed forests, which made solid land. With Dorothy headed in the right direction, Rachel could struggle to stay on her feet. The young cypress and blackgum trees crashed inwards as she fought for her footing on the gnarled twist of vines and grasses under her feet. What sounded like an army of animals scurried out of their way of their procession. Rachel squirmed at the thought of snakes. Finally, she screwed up her courage to ask Dorothy what was out there.

"I'm not sure, dear. Marsh rabbits, or rats,

maybe?"

Rats! Rachel picked her feet up higher and scampered more quickly toward solid ground.

"It's too bad the light is fading. There are several species of carnivorous plants that live in this swamp, and lots of other species — snapping turtles, bobcats, raccoons."

Rachel had a hard time reconciling a raccoon with its Zorro mask and her present surroundings. They seemed more suited to Elk Park.

As the women neared the tall cypress, bats emerged from the Spanish moss to feed on insects, swooping so close to their heads, Rachel thought she could feel the beat of their wings.

Then an alligator bellowed in the distance, and from somewhere close by, Rachel heard a squeal.

Just when she thought things couldn't get worse. Feral pigs.

Get a grip, Wilder. That was a legend.

One of Dwayne Carter's stories had been about pigs. How pigs had been turned loose in the swamp, and how over time they'd grown big and mean. The ending was that a man fed them "free" corn day after day, trapped them, and sold them at market. The moral was that "free" corn (a symbol for federal aid to farmers) cost the pigs (a symbol for the farmers) their lives (a symbol for freedom). His punch line had been, "The bacon you save may be your own." There weren't any feral pigs in the swamp.

So what creature had made the noise?

At last the ground hardened, and sand replaced the spongy ground. The shadows grew darker as the sun dipped low toward the marsh and tinged the clouds overhead in shades of red and pink. Lark collapsed at the base of an old pine, and Rachel prodded her to get up.

"There's no time to sit," she said. "It's going to be dark soon, and there's no telling what Dwight and Dwayne have done to Anderson and Wolcott."

"What I wouldn't give for a phone booth," said Lark.

The phone!

Rachel reached for the cell phone in her pocket, and flipped it open. One small bar edged up the outside.

A signal!

She punched the emergency speed dial.

"This is nine-one-one. Please state your emergency."

"I need to speak with Detective Stone."

"I'm sorry, you have reached nine-one-one dispatch. Please state your emergency."

"We are lost in the swamp, our canoe has been sunk, and two men are being held captive." Rachel waited for the dispatcher's reaction and got none.

"Please state your name and location."

"My name is Rachel Wilder, and I told you, we're lost in the swamp. We're in the Okefenokee National Wildlife Refuge, somewhere near Swamper's Island. Two men are being held hostage, and Dwight Carter sank our canoe."

"I'm sorry, you'll need to slow down. Start over."

"Please patch me through to Detective Stone," she said for the second time.

It took two supervisors and a triple-telling of the story, but eventually Detective Stone's voice pierced the static.

"Rachel?"

"Thank heavens." She repeated the story a fourth time, filling him in on the events of their birdwatching trip — about following Anderson and Wolcott through the prairies, about the men's intent to shoot the ivory-billed woodpecker, and about Dwight's sinking their boat.

"Do you have any idea where you are?"

"We were in the Mizel Prairie heading south to southeast when the canoe sank. We're on dry land now."

"Stay on the line. I'm going to see if we can get a triangulation off your cell phone signal and pinpoint your location."

It took close to five minutes before he came back. "You're about two hundred yards from the main road, halfway between the shortcut to Swamper's Island and the entrance to the Okefenokee Swamp Tour base. I want you to stay where you are. Stay in the woods and out of sight. We have help en route."

"How long will it take?" asked Rachel.

"Thirty minutes or so."

Rachel stared at the others. "Wolcott and Anderson might be dead by then."

"They might already be dead. Just stay where you are! Do you copy that?"

"I copy that." Rachel hung up and told the others what Detective Stone had said.

"Well, I vote we don't wait here," said Dorothy. "What if one of those Carter boys finds us? I think we should head back to the parking lot. It's barely after six o'clock. Evan Kearns wouldn't have left us."

"Of course he would, Dot. He made it clear we were to be back on the bus at five." Cecilia fluffed her hair. Mud streaked her face and her clothes, but she straightened the hem of her shirt and pulled up her socks. "You know the rules. If you miss the bus, then you're on your own."

Dorothy placed her hands on her hips. Her pants were soaked, and her long-sleeved light pink T-shirt looked tie-dyed with black. "This is different. It's a swamp trip, and it's nearly dark outside. Someone would have waited for us."

"Can we just rest here for a few minutes?" asked Lark.

The others flopped down beside her, their backs to the tree. They sat in silence, each absorbed in their own thoughts, each equally as frightened as she was, Rachel guessed.

"Get on your feet," said a voice. *A male voice.*

Rachel started to scramble up, then realized it was someone talking from the other side of the trees. Inching forward, she peeked through the thin trunks and realized she stood at the edge of the water separating the mainland from Swamper's Island. Two flashlight beams cut through the dusk, pointing a trail toward a rickety bridge. Dwight and Dwayne Carter shoved Victor Wolcott and Nevin Anderson ahead of them through the woods on the opposite side. Once they crossed the bridge, the women would be right in their path.

CHAPTER 19

"We have to get out of here," said Rachel, scrambling back to the others.

Lark sat up straighter. "Why? They're on the other side of the water, and Detective Stone told us to wait here."

"You don't understand. There's a bridge right there, and the Carter brothers are headed straight for it."

It didn't take any urging to get the others onto their feet. The light was dwindling, and the men's voices were growing louder.

Rachel struck out in the direction of the road, branches tearing at her ankles. The others followed, pressed so close at times she could feel hot breath on her neck and feared one of them might knock her over and trample her into the ground. Despite its lack of cover, reaching the road was a huge relief.

"Which way do we go?" whispered Lark.

"I *think*" — Rachel emphasized the word

— "that the turn off to the swamp tour headquarters is that direction." She pointed to her right.

"Then I say we go the opposite direction," said Lark.

Dorothy and Cecilia agreed.

Rachel nodded. "Just remember to stay close to the side of the road and be prepared to duck out of sight."

This time Rachel took up the rear. She could hear the rumble of the men's voices, and see an occasional flash of light, but so far the women appeared to be in the clear. After about a quarter of a mile, headlights appeared on the roadway headed in their direction.

The women leaped for the ditch, and flattened themselves on the ground.

"Do you think it's Detective Stone?" Cecilia asked.

Rachel glanced at her watch. "No, but it's not apt to be Fancy, either. She's probably back at headquarters and would be headed the other way."

"Let's flag them down," said Dorothy. She stood and stepped onto the road before Rachel could stop her, waving her arms over her head in the universal sign for "Stop."

The car slowed. It was a small green

Honda. Katie Anderson sat behind the wheel.

"Thank heavens, someone we know," said Cecilia pushing herself upright.

Lark jumped forward and yanked open the passenger-side door. "What are you doing here?"

"I came down to pick up my daddy," she said, a hesitation to her voice. "Is something wrong?"

"You might say that," said Dorothy, climbing into the back seat. Cecilia and Lark clambered in after her, leaving Rachel the front.

Katie pulled her purse into the middle. "Climb in."

"Your dad's in a lot of trouble," said Rachel. There wasn't time to break the news slowly, so Rachel blurted it out, explaining what had happened out in the swamp. "We've called Detective Stone, and he's due here soon, but . . ."

Katie didn't seem too worried. "Dwayne would never hurt my daddy."

"Did you not hear a word she said?" asked Lark. "He has him at gunpoint."

"It's not what you think."

Rachel didn't like how calm she was acting. "Is there something we should know?"

Reaching out for Katie's arm, Rachel's

hand struck Katie's purse. It gaped open, and she could see the cold edge of a steel film reel. A stab of fear shimmied from her heart to her throat. It was Katie who had taken the film, Katie who had pushed the threat underneath her door.

"How is it not what we think, Katie?" said Rachel.

Katie snatched up the purse and stuffed it under her legs. Her foot pressed on the accelerator and they lurched forward. "Daddy'll understand when he hears about the treasure."

"You think he's going to understand being marched by gunpoint through the swamp." Rachel was putting two and two together. "Dwayne's your baby's father, isn't he?"

Katie startled. "How did you know I was pregnant?"

"I overheard you arguing with your mom. But then, you knew that, didn't you? At the time I thought you were carrying Paul Becker's child."

Katie giggled. "That old fart? Not that he didn't try. I wasn't interested."

"You and your mom were fighting about your going to Sonja Becker. I thought you wanted child support, but you were after the film."

"Sonja Becker hates birdwatching about as much as my mother hates golf. It paid the bills, that's all. I figured she would happily give me the film if she had it, and I was right. It just turned out she didn't."

"Did Dwayne kill Becker?"

"No, that was his idiot brother."

They had reached the turn into the Okefenokee Swamp Tours headquarters, and Katie turned on her blinker. "Dwayne wanted to scare him, that's all. But Dwight was afraid he'd talk about the burial mound, and killed him instead."

Lark, Dorothy, and Cecilia sat wide-eyed in the back. Rachel saw Lark reach for the door handle, but Katie hit the door locks and held down the switch.

"Did he kill Knapp, too?" asked Rachel, her mind searching for options. They didn't have much time. The four of them could handle this little woman-child, but the men would be breaking out of the woods at any minute.

Katie pulled up next to Wolcott's car in the parking lot. Fancy's truck was gone, but Dwayne's truck was in the parking lot.

"He killed Knapp for the same reason," said Katie. "I figure he'll go gunning for Guy Saxby next."

"So what's to stop him from killing your

dad?" asked Rachel.

"We're family now. My daddy won't want to see his little girl go to jail for being an accessory to murder."

Daddy's little girl was no dummy, thought Rachel. Katie understood the hot water she was in. Still, she had that invincibility thing going on that teenagers tended to have. In her mind, nothing could happen to her. Rachel wondered when it was she had grown out of that. *Recently.*

She glanced at her watch. There were still fifteen minutes before Detective Stone's men were scheduled to arrive. A lot could happen in fifteen minutes.

A flashlight beam split the night, and Katie jumped out of the car, still holding her finger on the lock button. "Over here, Dwayne. I have them." Katie stuck her head back inside the car. "You're not the only one with a cell phone."

Rachel lunged forward, knocking Katie's finger off the door lock. She unlocked the car doors, and the four women tumbled out of the vehicle only to stare down the barrel of a gun.

"Over there." Dwight gestured with the gun, herding them into a tight little ball with the men.

"Hi, baby." Dwayne gave Katie a kiss, and

winked at Rachel over the top of her head. Rachel's stomach twisted. And to think she had once thought him cute, in a rogue sort of way.

"Katie?" whined her father. "Don't tell me you knew?"

"Of course I knew, Daddy. But it's okay now. Dwayne's going to let you go."

"The hell he is," said Dwight.

Katie fingers clutched at Dwayne's arm. "You tell him, Dwayne. He's my daddy, and he'll keep his mouth shut. Won't you, Daddy?"

Dwayne looked at Anderson, then back at Katie, and then he ducked his head sheepishly. "I'm sorry, baby. I'm afraid Dwight's right this time. Your daddy doesn't strike me as the forgetting type."

The realization that her boyfriend intended to kill her father contorted Katie's face. Tears began to stream down her cheeks. Clutching her stomach, she backed toward the car.

"Where's she goin'?" yelled Dwight, keeping the gun trained on the six of them. "Where do you think you're goin'? Damn it, Dwayne, she's got the film."

Dwayne's hand snaked out and grabbed Katie's wrist. Shoving her toward the group of hostages, he leaned inside the car, yanked the keys from the ignition, and rummaged through her purse. He held up the reel like a prize. "Get them all on the Maggie."

The "Maggie" turned out to be a white, flat-bottomed swamp boat that seated fifteen. Designed to travel in shallow water, it had a large airplane propeller on the back, with swivel seats for better viewing on the water. Dwight put the two men near the front, Dorothy and Cecilia opposite them, and Lark and Katie behind the men.

"You can't get away with this, Dwayne," said Rachel softly, waiting her turn to board. "Detective Stone is on his way. He knows everything. Dwight's the only one who has killed anyone so far."

"He's my brother," said Dwayne.

"And she's your girlfriend. She's carrying your baby."

"That was a mistake. I feel right bad about that."

Not bad enough to stop what was happening.

"What treasure is worth so many lives?"

Dwayne lit up at the word treasure. "We've been looking for that stash our whole lives, since we was little boys. Our pa always said it would be the only thing that could change our lives and get us out of this hellhole."

"Fancy was going to sell the land. You

300

would have made a fortune."

"Nothing like what's buried in that mound out there." Dwayne gestured toward the swamp. "Once Ma knows, she'll understand." He swept his arm like a gentlemen showing her the way aboard. "Need a hand?"

Rachel jerked her elbow out of his grasp and climbed onto the boat, sliding into a seat opposite Lark and Katie. Dwayne started the motor. While Dwight cast off, Rachel worked the cell phone out of her pocket and slipped it along the side of the seat into Cecilia's hand.

"They can track you by GPS," she whispered. "Keep it with you."

"Oh my, what are you going to do?" asked Cecilia.

"You two, shut up," ordered Dwight. "No talkin'."

As the boat started moving, Dwayne held up the reel and let the film play out into the water like fishing line. Dwight laughed, the deep belly laugh of someone who felt like he'd won, and a thousand pig frogs joined in the chorus. The two men cracked open beers, and Rachel inched toward the edge of the boat.

Waiting until they were both preoccupied with their celebration and the boat had reached the entrance to the canal, she launched herself into the water.

Dwight stopped laughing. "Shit! Where'd she go?"

He shone his flashlight into the water, and she bobbed under. The brackish liquid was dark, and over her head at this point. She worked her arms to stay under. So much for being able to stand up.

"Turn it around," yelled Dwight.

"I'm turning," said Dwayne. "Hold your horses."

The swamp boat was big, and Rachel figured it would take a bit of doing to turn it around in the canal. Dwayne would have to back it up a least once in order to swing it around. That should buy her at least thirty seconds.

She waited until she heard the motor roar, and then struck out for shore.

Dwight's light roamed the water.

The water was warm from the sun, but her blood ran cold when Dwight's light bounced off the tail of an alligator sliding into the water.

She was almost to shore. Another foot or two, and she would be on solid ground. Her foot struck bottom, and she ran for the trees.

The alligator slithered from the water behind her.

There was only one thing to do. Leaping into the air, she landed squarely on top of its snout.

It thrashed its tail trying to dislodge her, but she reached down, clamped its mouth together and hung on.

The gator bucked like a bronco. It twisted and jerked, then reared up on its front legs and swung its head side to side.

A shot rang out.

The alligator dropped, and lay still.

Another shot rang out.

Dwight had hit the gator, but the bullets were meant for her.

Jumping to her feet, she ran for the trees and sprinted toward the parking lot.

Detective Stone arrived just as she reached the cars, and the swamp boat was pulling back up to the dock. Dwayne and Dwight tried turning the boat around again, but Stone's men pinned them down with high-powered guns.

"My Lord, you look like you've been wrestling with an alligator," said Stone, once the brothers were in custody and screaming for their lawyer. "Are you okay?"

Rachel smiled weakly. "Nothing a tetanus shot, a hot bath, and a little sleep won't cure."

■ ■ ■ ■

She had gotten her wish, minus the shot. Lark had drawn her a bath, while Dorothy and Cecilia ordered room service. She had slept until the phone rang at nine. It was Detective Stone, wanting to know if the women wanted to accompany him to unbury a treasure. He figured they deserved a reward for all they'd been through.

And they weren't the only ones invited. Fancy and Dwayne Carter were there. As the primary shooter, Dwight was still behind bars, but Stone needed Dwayne's help finding the burial mound.

None of the Andersons or Victor Wolcott were there. In an emergency late-night vote, the Hyde Island Authority had removed Wolcott from the board and approved the land swap. Swamper's Island now belonged to the state. Katie was home under house arrest pending charges, but it appeared that Patricia and Nevin would get their golf course.

Guy Saxby had come calling the night before.

"You're a cheat, Guy," Dorothy had told him. "I cannot be with a man I cannot respect."

It had taken Rachel years to figure out what Dorothy had learned in a weekend. Based on Saxby's response, it was going to take him a lot longer than that.

The mound was under destruction when Rachel, Lark, Cecilia, and Dorothy arrived. Dwayne stood off to one side in handcuffs waiting for the deputies to hit pay dirt. He studied the activity like he still stood to gain from the booty.

"What were you boys thinking?" Fancy asked him. "How could you screw up like this?"

They had more than screwed up, thought Rachel. They had murdered two people, and attempted to kill seven others. It was of small comfort to know they would have been caught.

Fancy blew her nose. She looked her age today, and then some. Her bright blue eye shadow only accentuated the redness and puffiness of her face. "You've ruined everything."

"It's the treasure, Ma," said Dwayne. He gestured with his arms, holding them out in front of him and jingling the cuffs. "It's here, just like Pa said."

"Your pa was an alcoholic, and crazier than a loon." Fancy belted him on the shoulder. "We had a good thing going. We

305

were going to sell the land and move into Brunswick, buy us a nice house."

"Ma, with this treasure we can buy five nice houses."

"Not anymore, son."

"I think we've got something, sir," one of the deputies shouted.

It took a little more digging and two deputies to drag the strongbox free of the mound. It measured thirteen inches by nine inches by seven inches tall and was decorated with an ornate design.

"It fits Aponi Carter's era," said Detective Stone. "Though where she would have laid her hands on one of these we'll never know."

"They were used on stagecoaches," said Dorothy. "Maybe one ended up in the swamp."

"Open it," said Dwayne. He had edged closer, his guard on his tail.

The deputy who had unearthed it reached for a pry bar, and torqued open the lid. Glass beads spilled onto the ground along with several glass rings, and a rosary made of coral. Inside several old iron tools were nestled in rotting cloth.

"There's got to be more in there than that," said Dwight.

The deputy dug deeper. "Wait. Here's something."

He came up with a brass plaque. It was embossed with the image of a king, and inscribed across the bottom were the words, *King Felipe II, Don Carlos de Hapsburg.*

"He was the King of Spain at the time of the conquistadors," said Dorothy.

"That's it," said Dwayne, his voice rising in anger. "That's the treasure?"

"It looks like it," said Detective Stone. "Doesn't seem worth it now, does it?"

"Well, it's got to be worth something," said Dorothy. "A few thousand dollars."

Everyone stared at her.

Kent.

"Did you hear that?" asked Cecilia.

"Hear what?" Dorothy cocked her head to listen.

Kent.

"It sounds like a clarinet, or a child's horn," said Lark.

"That's the call of the ivory-billed woodpecker," said Rachel.

Kent.

"How do you know that?" asked Lark.

"I looked it up on the Internet."

"It could be the pileated," said Dorothy.

"No, their call is different. The ivory-billed's call is softer, and has characteristic pauses between the notes." Rachel wished she had thought to bring her binoculars. At least Dorothy, Cecilia, and Lark had remembered. "Look in the trees. They don't call in flight."

Everyone was listening now.

Kent. Kent. Kent.

"Who cares about a bird?" said Dwayne.

The deputy yanked on his cuffs, and he fell quiet.

Suddenly a large bird swooped from the trees. It was a female, but the black and white of the wings were unmistakable. It lit on a tree at the edge of the clearing. Rachel pulled her camera phone out of her pocket, focused, and shot. She recorded three pictures before the bird flew away.

"We have to call the hotline," said Cecilia.

"No," said Dorothy. "We need to call the state. The last thing we want is a horde of birders descending on the island and disturbing the birds."

"I agree with Dorothy," said Lark. "What do you think, Rae?"

Rachel stared at the photographs on her camera phone. "I need to e-mail Kirk."

PAINTED BUNTING
PASSERINA CIRIS
FAMILY: FRINGILLIDAE

APPEARANCE: A small, beautiful bird, the male painted buntings are the most spectacularly colored of all North American songbirds, with a gaudy combination of red, blue, and green feathers. He has a blue head, a green back, a dark red nape, and red underparts, rump, and eye ring. The females are plain green with no markings.

RANGE: Painted buntings have two distinct breeding populations. The eastern population — found along the Atlantic Coast from North Carolina south to central Florida — winters in southern Florida and the northwestern Caribbean. The western population — covering much of Louisiana, Arkansas, Oklahoma, Texas, and southward into northern Mexico — winters in southern Mexico and Central America.

HABITAT: The painted bunting favors somewhat open areas with dense brush at all seasons. A fan of the southeastern thickets, males often sing from perches well hidden among foliage in low trees.

VOICE: Painted buntings have a bright fast warble, *graffiti graffiti spaghetti-for-two.*

BEHAVIORS: Males defend their territory by singing from a high perch, often hidden among the uppermost foliage of a tree. Males, who may have more than one mate, will actually fight to hold territories. These fights are sometimes bloody and even fatal.

CONSERVATION: The painted bunting diet consists mostly of seeds and insects, with insects predominating during the breeding season. There has been a significant decline in the numbers of painted buntings over the past thirty-five years. While the exact cause is unknown, it is most likely related to habitat. Both the eastern and western populations have been negatively impacted by an increase in land development resulting in the degradation or destruction of habitat. Cowbird parasitism may also be impacting the eastern population. Finally, because of their spectacular appearance, male painted buntings are popular as cage birds, and thousands are taken annually in Mexico and Central

America for export to bird dealers in Europe.

ABOUT THE AUTHOR

Christine Goff lives in Colorado with her husband, three of her six children, three dogs, and various wildlife — her inspiration for murder. *Death Shoots a Birdie* is the fifth novel in the Birdwatcher's Mystery series. Visit her Web site at http://www.christine goff.com.

The employees of Thorndike Press hope you have enjoyed this Large Print book. All our Thorndike and Wheeler Large Print titles are designed for easy reading, and all our books are made to last. Other Thorndike Press Large Print books are available at your library, through selected bookstores, or directly from us.

For information about titles, please call:
(800) 223-1244

or visit our Web site at:
www.gale.com/thorndike
www.gale.com/wheeler

To share your comments, please write:
Publisher
Thorndike Press
295 Kennedy Memorial Drive
Waterville, ME 04901